DATE DUE

JUL 1	1974		
MAR. 7	1975		
FEB. 2 2 1982			
JUL 3 1 1982			
JAN 0 7 2004			

Fairy Tales from Bohemia

Fairy Tales from Bohemia

Retold by
MAURICE AND PAMELA MICHAEL

Illustrated by
JOHN LATHEY

FOLLETT PUBLISHING COMPANY
Chicago *New York*

Library of Congress Catalog Card Number: 68-13804

First Printing

Follett Publishing Company
1010 West Washington Boulevard
Chicago, Illinois 60607

T/L 2410

Contents

Illustrations

ONE

The Sun-Horse

ONCE, LONG, LONG AGO, there was a country upon which, for some strange reason, the sun had stopped shining. There, the days were as black as the night and all was dark and gloomy and sad. Those who lived in the country would have left and gone to live elsewhere, abandoning their houses and farms to the owls and bats and other creatures of the night, if their King had not had the good fortune to possess a horse with a white blaze on its forehead that gave out light, just like the real sun. So, to enable people to go on living in his domains, the King had his groom lead this wonder-horse throughout the length and breadth of his kingdom. And where the horse was, all was as bright as on midsummer's day, but elsewhere all was dark.

Then one day there was a tremendous outcry and commotion: the horse had disappeared. Darkness lay over the entire country, evil and oppressive, darkness so black that people could not work or till the ground. No one could work or trade; and people were afraid and unhappy, and they murmured that this would not do, that if the King could not provide light, they would have to go to some other country and live under a different King who could. The King realised that he must make a great effort, so he mobilised the army and organised a nation-wide search.

In a long thin line they groped their way through the darkness till they came to the frontier, where a different country began. Here there were woods and forest with trees a thousand years old and more, and above them was the sun struggling through a layer of mist. Undaunted, the King and his army plunged in among these aged trees, continuing their search. After a short while, the King came to a very humble-looking cottage standing all by itself. The King walked inside, wanting to ask where they were and if the people there had seen any sign of his horse, but he had no need to ask. Inside the hut, he saw a table at which sat a middle-aged man reading a great book. At the King's greeting, the man looked up, then got to his feet. The man was tall and there was something about his features and his whole bearing that told the King that here was no ordinary man.

'I was just reading about you,' said the man. 'You're looking for the sun-horse, I take it? It's a waste of time, because you would never be able to get it, even if you could find it; but I will get it for you. Leave everything to me and go back home. You are needed there. And take your army with you. I won't need it; but leave me one man as an orderly.'

'All right,' said the King. 'I'll reward you richly, if you can bring me back the sun-horse.'

'I ask for no reward. Just go back home, where you are needed, and leave me in peace to make my preparations.'

So the King and the whole army turned round and marched back the way they had come, through the gloom of their dark and stricken land, while the Seer, for such was the man who lived in that lonely cottage, went back to his book and read until late into the night.

The next day, the Seer and his orderly set out from the cottage. They had a long way to go, through six countries they went and even farther, but in the seventh country they saw a kingly palace and halted a little way from it. This country was ruled by three brutal brothers who had married three sisters, the daughters of a nasty, old witch called Striga, who lived in the palace with them. Then the Seer said to his orderly:

'You stay here, while I go to the palace and find out if the Kings are at home.'

The next moment the Seer transformed himself into a green bird; then he flew to the palace and up to the bay window of the room in which the eldest of the three Queens was sitting. There he fluttered about and pecked at the glass with his beak, until the Queen came and opened the window and let him in. He flew about and alighted on the Queen's hand and shoulder and was so sweet and tame that the Queen thought he was quite the nicest thing she had ever seen and exclaimed:

'What a pity the King is away; because he would love you too, I'm sure. But he will be back this evening from inspecting his third of the kingdom.'

Then she went on playing with the bird.

Suddenly the door opened and in came the Queen's mother, the witch Striga, and the moment she saw the bird, she cried out:

'Wring its neck! Wring that bird's neck, else blood will be shed.'

'What do you mean?' said the Queen. 'This dear innocent little bird. Look how sweet he is!'

But the witch answered:

'False innocence, that's what it is! Give that bird to me, and I'll wring its neck!'

And she hurried across the floor towards her daughter.

At this the Seer wisely turned himself into a man, ran to the door and dashed out, before the two women had recovered from their surprise.

Outside, the Seer turned himself back into a green bird and flew straight to the window of the middle sister and pecked and fluttered at it till she, too, came and opened the window and let the bird in. The bird at once perched on her white hand and looked at her so sweetly. Then it ran up her arm and hopped on to her shoulder, and round the back of her neck to her other shoulder, and was altogether so pretty and entrancing that the Queen exclaimed:

'Oh, what a pity the King's away. I'm sure he would love you, too. But he'll be back tomorrow evening after inspecting his third of the kingdom.'

Then, suddenly, the door opened and the witch Striga appeared. Catching sight of the bird, her face paled and she called out:

'Catch that bird! Wring its neck. It'll do you harm.'

'Do me harm!' retorted the Queen. 'This sweet, innocent little bird?'

'Innocent my foot,' cried the witch. 'Give that bird to me!' and she rushed forward, hand outstretched to seize the bird. But again the Seer turned himself back into a person and opened the door and darted out, before either of the two women realised what was happening.

The moment he was safe outside the palace once more, the Seer again turned himself into a green bird and flew to the window of the youngest of the three sisters. Here again he fluttered and pecked at the glass until the young Queen came and opened the casement and let him in. The little green bird at once began to make a fuss of her, hopping about her shoulders, rubbing its head against her cheek and making sweet, low chirruping noises, that the young Queen was quite entranced and exclaimed:

'Oh, what a pity my husband won't be back till the day after tomorrow and then not till the evening, because he would love you too.'

Then the door flew open with a bang and in rushed the queen's mother, the old witch Striga. Seeing the green bird, as she had feared, she cried out:

'There's that bird again. Wring its neck or it'll do you harm."

'Do me harm, Mother! This sweet innocent little bird!' said the Queen.

'Not so innocent as you think. Give it to me,' said the witch, stretching out her skinny old hand.

Immediately the Seer turned himself back into a man and plunged through the door and out. And search the palace though they did, there was not a sign of him to be seen anywhere. This, of course, was because he was outside the walls with his orderly, for, now that he knew where the three kings were, he did not need to stay in the city any longer. However, he sent his orderly in to buy food for three days and arranged to meet him at the bridge that carried the only road to the city across the great river, and which the three Kings would have to cross on their way home. There, as soon as the orderly returned, they made themselves a camp beneath the bridge and settled down to wait.

Towards evening, when the sun seemed to be resting on the tops of the trees, they heard the hollow sound of horse's hooves on the bridge: the eldest of the Kings was returning home. Half-way across, the King's horse stumbled over a plank and the king exclaimed:

'To the gallows with the incompetent fool who built this bridge!'

At this, the Seer leaped out from beneath the bridge and rushed at the King, shouting:

'How dare you curse an innocent person like that!'

Then the Seer drew his sword and the King drew his, but he could not stand up to the tremendous blows dealt him by the Seer and, after a brief struggle, he toppled from his horse dead. Then the Seer picked the King's body up, slung it over his horse, tied it on and, with a smack on the rump, sent the horse cantering off to the city. And so the dead King was brought home.

The Seer then returned to his hide-out under the bridge, where he stayed until the following evening. Then, as the sun was again pricking itself on the tops of the trees, the second King came riding home. His horse's hooves rang hollowly on the bridge, then stopped as the King reined in when he caught sight of the blood on the bridge.

'Somebody's been killed here,' said the King. 'What rascal has had the impertinence to usurp my royal prerogative?'

At that, the Seer leaped out from under the bridge and rushed with drawn sword at the King, shouting:

'How dare you abuse me! Defend yourself, if you can. You are about to die!'

The King tried to defend himself, but he was no match for the Seer and after a brief fight, he toppled off his horse, dead. The Seer lifted him back, tied him on again and giving the horse a smack with the flat of his sword, sent it galloping off to the city, carrying the dead body of its second King.

Once more the Seer returned to his hide-out under the bridge, where he and his orderly spent another uncomfortable night and a boring day. That evening, when the sun was already below the trees and the Seer was beginning to wonder, he heard the sound of rapid hoof beats. The third and youngest King was returning, riding the sun-horse itself, which he was urging along because he was late. However, when he saw the blood on the bridge, he reined in and exclaimed:

'What rogue has dared to deprive my royal arm of a victim?'

Scarcely had he spoken, before the Seer was on the bridge advancing towards him with drawn sword.

'Hallo!' said the King and drew his sword.

Then began a fight that would have gone down in history, if any one had been there to see it. The King and the Seer seemed evenly matched, despite the latter's magic powers, and neither could break the other's defence. On and on they fought till the sweat was running down their faces, then their swords met in a more violent clash than ever before and both blades smashed.

'We can't do any more with our swords,' said the

Then began a fight that would have gone down in history . . .

Seer, 'let's turn ourselves into wheels and roll down that hill. Whoever is smashed is the loser.'

'All right,' said the King. 'I'll be a wagon-wheel.'

'Wait a bit!' said the Seer. 'You be what you like, but I'm the wagon-wheel.'

The King agreed, so the two walked up to the top of the hill, there turned themselves into wheels and set off rolling down hill. The wagon-wheel bounced, then gave a bound, crashed into the other wheel and broke it. The Seer turned back into himself again and exclaimed triumphantly:

'There! I've won!'

'Not yet, friend,' said the King, appearing in front of the Seer. 'You've only broken my little finger. I know, let's turn ourselves into flames and whichever burns the other is the winner. I'll be a red flame, so you be a white.'

'Not so quickly,' said the Seer. 'I'll be the red flame, you the white.'

The King had to agree to this so, there on the road, near the bridge, they turned themselves into flames and began trying to burn each other. For a long time neither seemed able to make an impression on the other, then an old beggar came along. He had a long dirty, white beard and a bald head, and a huge satchel at his side and a stout staff.

'Hallo, old man,' called the white flame, 'get some water and pour it over that red flame and I'll give you a penny.'

But the red flame went one better and offered the beggar a shilling to pour water over the white flame and naturally the beggar preferred a shilling to a penny, so he filled his cap with water at the bridge and emptied it over the white flame, which hissed and sizzled for a moment and went out, leaving the Seer the winner. He at once turned back into himself, caught the sun-horse's bridle, gave the beggar his shilling and calling for his orderly, mounted the sun-horse and rode away.

Meanwhile, there was a commotion in the palace and loud mourning over the two dead Kings and anxious wondering why the third had not yet returned. The old witch, Striga, roamed restlessly from room to room, then all at once she seemed to come to a decision: going to a cupboard under the stairs she produced a broom, jumped on to it and taking her daughters by the hand, soared off with them into the air.

The Seer and his orderly had got quite a way, for they were hurrying, afraid of Striga and what she might do. They were in a desolate bit of country and feeling very hungry, for the orderly had only bought food for three days and they had already eaten all of it. At last they came to an apple-tree, its branches heavy with red fruit that had the most delicious smell. 'Thank goodness,' said the orderly. 'I can eat a few of those.' But the Seer was suspicious and drawing his sword, hacked at the trunk and at once blood poured out.

'There,' he exclaimed, 'if you eat any of those apples they will destroy you. That tree is the eldest Queen, whom the witch has planted there to tempt us.'

They rode on, getting more and more hungry and thirsty. After a while, they came to a well.

'Well, if I can't have apples, a good long drink will at least be something,' said the orderly. But the Seer forbade him to drink; then he plunged his sword into the water, which at once became stained with blood. 'That water would have poisoned you,' said the Seer. 'It's the second Queen, whom the witch has put there to trap us.'

After a while, they came to where a rose-bush was standing all by itself, covered with the loveliest and most fragrant roses. Most suspicious, thought the Seer, but the simple orderly would have rushed up and picked some, if the Seer had not held him back. Then he slashed at the bush with his sword and blood spattered the ground. 'That was the third Queen,' said the Seer.

So they journeyed on. After a while the Seer said:

'We're over the worst now, because we are outside Striga's territory, but we can't assume we're safe. She may try all sorts of things yet.'

Scarcely had he spoken the words than they saw a small boy walking along, holding a bridle in his hand.

As he drew abreast, the boy dived under the sun-horse, touching its belly with the bridle. The sun-horse reared, throwing the Seer and the boy leaped into the saddle and galloped off.

'What did I tell you,' said the Seer.

'What a dirty trick,' cried the orderly. 'We'll have to catch them.'

'Leave that to me,' said the Seer. 'You carry on and and wait for me at the boundary of your master's terri-tory. I'll catch you up there.'

So the Seer hurried after the sun-horse and its youthful rider and soon caught them up, when he assumed the disguise of an ordinary countryman.

'Where do you come from?' asked the boy-sorcerer.

'From far away.'

'And where are you going?'

'Looking for work.'

'Come and look after my horse. I'll pay you well.'

'Well, why not,' said the countryman and so the Seer became the sorcerer's servant, though the sorcerer did not realise whom he was employing, his mind being rather pre-occupied with a certain girl he was trying to persuade to marry him. The girl was kept prisoner in a castle on an island in a big lake. One day the sorcerer asked the Seer to go and try and persuade her to come and visit him. The Seer got a boat and rowed across to the girl's island. There he said he was a pedlar and had lots of fine things to show, and he magically produced a lot of ribbons, materials and buckles, and the girl came and sat in the boat to look at it all. The Seer pushed off and they were at the other bank before the girl looked up and saw that the pedlar was rowing. Then she agreed to visit the sorcerer and the Seer told her that if she could find out where the sorcerer got his power from, he would see that she became free.

So the girl was very kind to the sorcerer who was so besotted with her, and when she asked him where he got his power from, he told her; in a hollow in a big tree in the forest is a duck's egg and my power is in that.

That was all the Seer needed to know. He hurried to the forest, soon found a big tree with a hollow in it and there saw a duck's egg. He took the egg and drank it off raw, and went back to the house, where, to his delight, he found that the sorcerer had become an old, old man, as feeble as a baby. Then he said good-bye to the girl, mounted the sun-horse and rode away.

He reached the boundary of the King's dominions at the same time as the orderly, and together they journeyed on. The sun-horse spread light and warmth wherever it passed, so that the crops began to grow again and the people could work and be happy. The King was overjoyed to get his sun-horse back and wanted to reward the Seer with half his kingdom, but the Seer did not want to rule or command. He liked living in his lonely cottage deep in the age-old forest with his books, and hurried back there as fast as he could.

TWO

The Haunted Mill

THERE WAS ONCE a haunted mill, set beside a deep, dark mill-pool. It had been deserted for many years, the big water-wheel had rotted half away and long streamers of weed, like green hair, hung from its slats. There were holes in the roof and the wind blew through the gaps in its walls. No one came there, except the swallows, to build their nests on its beams in the summer, and the bad old water-sprite who haunted it.

One day of pouring rain, a small travelling circus came to the neighbourhood, and the owner sought the shelter of the old mill for his animals. In fact, he decided to spend the night there. He had just got his animals settled, when the water-sprite appeared, carrying a basket full of fishes. He was a hideous sight, with a grey, shiny skin and lank, greenish hair, like the weed on the water-wheel. The circus man had made a fire to warm himself by, and some of his monkeys were huddled round it, drying their fur. The water-sprite sat down by the fire, too, as though he had every right to be there, and started to fry his fishes in a pan. When he thought they were nearly done, he stabbed one on his fork and tasted it, and one of the monkeys

He was a hideous sight, with grey, shiny skin and lank, greenish
hair

stretched out its paw to ask for a piece for itself. The water-sprite let out a terrible yell and struck the monkey's paw with his fork, and the poor animal had such a fright that all its fur stood on end and it fled. After a few minutes, another monkey stretched out its paw, but received the same treatment and backed away from the fire, chattering with fright.

Now the circus man had a performing bear in his troupe, and it had been watching all this from a little way off. When it saw its friends, the monkeys, treated like this, it rose up on its hind legs and waddled slowly towards the fire. He, too, stretched out a large paw towards the pan of fish and the water-sprite let out a hair-raising scream and whacked the bear across the nose. This was more than the bear would stand. It seized the water-sprite in its strong arms and squeezed and squeezed him. The water-sprite wriggled and twisted in the bear's grasp, but though he was as slippery as an eel, the bear was too strong for him and at last his struggles ceased and he fell to the ground, dead.

The circus man threw the water-sprite's body into the mill-stream and it was carried swiftly away, never to be seen again. Then he and the animals gathered round the fire and finished off the fish, which were done to a turn.

That was how the circus bear rid the mill of its evil spirit after which it was no longer a gloomy place where people feared to go.

THREE

Why Dogs Hate Cats

ONCE A LONG, long time ago, when the earth was very much younger, all the kings of the world met in council, and after deliberating for many weeks, announced that they were granting dogs their royal charter and that henceforth they alone should have the privilege of accompanying man on all his goings and his comings, guarding his house and property and helping him in all the different things that he did. The dogs, of course, were immensely proud at being favoured in this way, but the cats were green with jealousy.

Then the cats held a general assembly at which it was decided that they would try to steal the dogs' charter and so deprive them of it. And that is exactly what they did. How they did it, or when, I do not know, and it is really neither here nor there, but the fact remains that the great parchment on which the charter was inscribed came into possession of the cats, who, with much miaowing and spitting dragged it up to the attic of a certain house and stuffed it under a pile of junk and rubbish there. And there a mouse found it, while searching for food. The mouse hurried joyfully back to its fellow to report its wonderful discovery. The mice, realising the value of the find, held council and debated how best to preserve this precious document, the possession of which would surely give them power over cats and dogs alike. They argued this way and that, and for a long time could reach no decision; then, finally, the eldest of them all, a bowed old she-mouse with a silvery muzzle and scarred tail, stood up and said:

'Fellow mice! After long consideration it seems to me that the only safe way of preventing the precious document from again falling into the hands of the cats, will be to eat it. Do that, and we shall have it in our power and will have no need to fear it being taken from us.' This suggestion pleased everybody and without delay they trooped in a body to the attic and feasted on the parchment of the dogs' charter, of which not so much as a particle was left uneaten by the time they had finished.

Some time later, the dogs decided to hold a meeting and ordered their archivist to produce the royal charter, so that new members might see and admire it. Then the archivist had to confess that it had been stolen by the cats, as he had recently established. Immediately they heard this the dogs went for the cats in a rage and told them to produce the charter or else! At first, the cats lied and tried to pretend that they had never taken it and had not got it, but being pressed by the dogs, they finally admitted that they had taken it and said that they would give it back.

So, the cats went to the attic where they had hidden the charter only to find that it had vanished, but everything round about smelt so strongly of mouse and so many mouse footprints were there, that there was no doubt who had taken it. The mice also tried to deny having taken it, but, as the cats pointed out, no one but they had access to the attic except the cats themselves. Eventually the mice had to confess that they were responsible for the charter's disappearance and also that they were unable to give it back, since, on the advice of their senior councillor, they had eaten it.

You can understand what the dogs felt, when they heard this, and that is why, ever since, dogs have hated cats with a bitter hatred and pursued them and harried them whenever they could, and why cats wage eternal warfare on mice, and kill and eat them whenever they can.

FOUR

The Iron Castle

ONCE UPON A TIME there was a King. His was only a small kingdom, but he liked being its King and wanted his family to go on ruling it. But the King was worried, because he had just one son and the son showed no sign of wanting to get married. One day, the King sent for his son and said:

'Son, it really is time you got married. Don't you know any girl you would like to marry?'

'That's just it,' said the Prince. 'There isn't one, or I haven't met her yet. There aren't a great many princesses round here, you know.'

'Well, perhaps I can help,' said the King, and, feeling in his pocket, he produced a golden key and held it out to his son. 'Go to the top of the tower, open the door in the ceiling and go in. Perhaps you will find what you are looking for there.'

This sounded very mysterious. The Prince had often wondered what was behind that door, which was always locked. Now he was going to see. Taking the key, he walked up many flights of stairs till he came to the iron door at the top. Fitting the key into the lock, he opened the door and climbed inside.

It was a big, round room. The ceiling was blue, the

colour of the clear night sky, studded with silver stars, and on the floor was a green silken carpet. Cut into the walls were twelve tall windows in golden niches. On the glass of each one was the picture of a different girl, in glorious robes and with a crown on her head. Each girl was more lovely than the last, so lovely that the Prince could scarcely take his eyes off them. As he looked the girls began to move, or so it seemed: they looked at him, smiled and did everything but speak. Then the Prince noticed that one of the windows was curtained. Drawing the curtains aside, he saw another picture of a girl dressed in white, with a silver belt, and a crown of pearls on her head. She, he thought, was the loveliest of them all, yet her face was pale and sad. The Prince stood for a long time gazing at her and as he looked, he fell in love and whispered to himself, 'This is the one I shall marry.' As he said that, the girl blushed and bowed her head, then all the pictures vanished.

The Prince hurried back to his father and told him about the girls he had seen. The King looked grave when he heard which one it was the Prince wanted to marry.

'You were wrong to uncover what was veiled,' he said, 'and your choice is going to run you into danger, because that girl is in the power of a wicked sorcerer, who keeps her prisoner in an iron castle. No one who has tried to free her has ever returned from there; but as you have chosen her, you, too must go and try.'

So, the next day the Prince mounted his horse and set out alone in search of his bride. On and on he rode, and entered a great forest plunging deeper and deeper into it, until he was in a part where he had never been before. Then he heard someone calling and looking round, he saw a tall man hurrying after him.

'Give me a job. Take me on as your servant and I promise you won't regret it,' said the tall man.

Now, as the Prince had no one with him and was feeling rather lost, he thought this might be a good idea, and so he asked the man what his name was and what he could do.

'My name is Long,' said the tall man, 'and I am very good at reaching things. Do you see that bird's nest in that tall fir-tree there? I'll reach up and get it for you.'

Then the tall man's body began to stretch and stretch until it was as tall as the fir-tree, he reached for the nest, and having got it, shrank rapidly until he was his former size, when he handed the nest to the prince.

'That was very clever,' said the Prince, 'but I would think you cleverer still if you would get me out of this forest.'

'Oh, that's easy,' said Long, and he began to stretch and stretch till he was three times the height of the tallest tree, then he looked all round and, pointing, said: 'If we go in this direction, we shall be out of the forest in no time.' Then he shrank until he was his former size, took the Prince's horse by the bridle and strode off in the direction in which he had pointed.

Before long the trees began to thin out, and soon the two men emerged on to a wide plain bounded in the distance by grey cliffs and wooded mountains. Away in the distance was the figure of a man.

Then the tall man's body began to stretch until it was as tall as
the fir tree

'Hello,' said Long, 'there's a friend of mine. You ought to give him a job too. He would be most useful.'

'Call him, then, and let me see him,' said the Prince.

'It's rather far for him to hear, I think I had better step across,' said Long and stretching himself up, till his head was lost in the clouds, he took a couple of steps, picked up his friend and put him down in front of the Prince.

Long's friend was a dumpy little man with an enormous paunch.

'Who are you and what do you do?' asked the Prince.

'My name's Broad,' said the man, 'and broaden is what I do.'

'Broaden,' said the Prince in surprise. 'What do you mean?'

'I'll show you, sir,' said Broad.

'Quick, Master, ride for the wood,' shouted Long.

The Prince could not understand what he meant, but seeing Long running helter-skelter, he dug his spurs into his horse and galloped after him. And he was only just in time, for Broad was already swelling so fast that he would have crushed the Prince, horse and all, if he had not galloped away.

Having shown what he could do, Broad blew out the air with which he had puffed himself up and the force of it bent the trees double and would have blown Long and the Prince away, if Broad had not been facing the other way.

'Well,' said the Prince, when Broad had regained his normal size, 'I'm not likely to meet anyone else who can do that, so you had better come and serve me too.'

Then the three of them continued on their way across the plain. As they approached the grey cliffs, they saw another figure.

'Hello! There's our friend Sharp Eyes,' cried Broad and Long together. Then the Prince saw that the man's eyes were bandaged.

'Why do you walk along with your eyes bandaged, so that you cannot see where you are going?' asked the Prince.

'But I can see perfectly well,' the man replied. 'My eyes are so sharp that I can see as well with a bandage over them as ordinary people can without. If I take this bandage off, I look right through everything and my gaze is so hot that things catch fire or, if they can't burn, they split and break into pieces.'

To demonstrate his powers, Sharp Eyes removed his bandage and fixed his gaze on a rock. The rock at once began to crackle and bits flew off it in all directions. Before long, there was nothing left but a heap of fine dust in the midst of which something glittered and sparkled. Sharp-Eyes walked across, picked the thing up and handed it to the prince. It was a lump of pure gold.

'By Jove!' said the Prince. 'I would be a fool not to engage you.'

The Prince then told them of his quest and asked them to help him, which they gladly promised to do. First, Sharp Eyes had to look and see how far it was to the Iron Castle and what was going on there. He reported that they would reach the Castle by nightfall and that the people there were busy preparing supper for them. The girl the Prince wanted to marry was in a room at the top of a tall tower with iron bars across the window.

On they journeyed and as the sun dropped low in the sky, the hills through which they had been travelling gradually got smaller and smaller, and then at last they came to another plain, in which loomed the Iron Castle.

The sun was just disappearing as the four men stepped off the iron drawbridge that led across the red-brown dirty waters of the moat into the castle. As it disappeared below the horizon, the heavy drawbridge began to rise, seemingly by itself, and the gates closed behind the new-comers with a bang, shutting them in. They halted in the great courtyard and waited. No one came. They looked about them. There wasn't a sign of anyone. And there wasn't a sound to be heard.

Seeing a door, the Prince went across and peeped inside. It led into a stable, to a stall with food and water all ready prepared for a horse. The Prince led his horse in, removed its saddle and bridle, rubbed it down and saw that it was comfortable, then he went back to the others. The four men then walked through another, larger doorway into the castle hall itself. This was deserted too, and so were all the other rooms through which they went. The rooms were furnished and crowded with people, nobles, ladies and servants, but they had all been turned to stone and remained motionless, with dust on their heads and shoulders and outstretched arms. Finally, the prince and his companions came to the great dining-hall. Here, the light had been lit, the table laid with four places and covered with steaming dishes of delicious-smelling food and bottles of wine. They waited and waited, their mouths watering, hoping that someone would come and invite them to eat. In the end, they could restrain themselves no longer, but sat down and began to eat and drink.

Having finished their meal, they began to wonder where they were going to sleep. Just as Broad was stifling a yawn, the door flew open with a bang and a moment or two later, a hump-backed old man with a bald head, grey whiskers and a beard that reached to his knees, stepped into the room. The man wore a long black robe fastened with three iron hoops round his waist in place of a belt and by the hand he led a girl. She was dressed all in white, with a crown of pearls on her hair and a silver belt round her slim waist, and her face was pale and sad. The Prince knew her at once. She was the girl he had seen in the room in his father's tower. He leaped to his feet and went towards her, but before he could speak, the old man, who was a sorcerer, said:

'I know who you are and why you have come. You want to take this girl away. All right, if you can watch over her for three nights, so that she does not escape from you, you can take her away. But if she does escape, you and your servants will be turned to stone, like all the others here.'

The Prince just nodded. He could not take his eyes off the girl. The old man led her to a chair and walked out, leaving her sitting there.

The Prince spoke to the girl. She did not reply. He began asking her questions, but she neither answered him nor smiled. She did not even move, and, if he had not seen her walk, he would have thought that she too had been turned to stone. The Prince felt desperately sorry for her and was quite determined to rescue her. So, to make sure that she did not escape, Long stretched himself till his body lay all round the walls of the room and Broad settled himself by the door and puffed himself out, completely blocking it. Sharp Eyes took up position in the middle of the room, on guard, and the Prince sat down determined to keep awake all night.

After a short time, however, their eyes closed; they just could not keep awake and they all slept until nearly morning.

The Prince was the first to wake, just before dawn. He opened his eyes and saw to his horror that the girl had gone. Cursing himself, he leaped to his feet and quickly roused the others. Seeing his despair, Sharp Eyes said:

'Don't worry, sir. I'll soon find her.'

Then he gazed intently out of the window. A few moments later, he exclaimed:

'Ah, there she is! A hundred miles from here is a big wood with an old oak growing in the middle of it. The oak is covered with acorns and the topmost acorn is the girl. Let Long take me on his shoulders and we'll soon get her for you.'

So, Sharp Eyes climbed on to Long's back, and Long stretched himself till his every step covered ten miles so that in less time than it takes to tell, they were back with the acorn. The Prince took it in his hand and then at Long's suggestion, dropped it on the ground, when the girl was suddenly standing before him.

As the young prince stood gazing at the girl, the sun rose above the hills, the door of the room flew open with a crash and the old man walked in, a wicked smile on his lips. When he saw the girl, his smile vanished and he scowled. There was a loud crack and one of the iron hoops round his waist snapped and fell to the ground. Then the old man took the girl by the hand and led her away.

All that day the Prince and his companions roamed about the castle and its grounds, where everything was dead and nothing moved. There were people in the rooms, horses in the stables, but all turned to stone: some in the act of eating, fork raised to open mouth, goblet at parted lips, some had been walking or running, and all frozen in the attitude of what they had been doing, when the sorcerer had cast his spell.

At lunch-time another splendid meal appeared for them in the dining-hall, and when they returned there in the evening it was to find a further feast awaiting them. The silver spoons heaped the food on their plates without being touched, and the wine poured itself out. When they had finished, the door opened and in came the old man with the girl for the Prince to guard a second night.

Whether it was that the wine was drugged or a spell had been laid upon them, try as they did to keep awake, the Prince and his three companions were quite unable to do so and were soon sound asleep. Just before dawn, the Prince awoke and seeing that the girl was no longer in her chair, he took Sharp Eyes by the shoulder and shook him awake.

'We've all been asleep, Sharp Eyes, and she's

gone,' said the Prince. 'Perhaps you can see where she is.'

Sharp Eyes went to the window, removed the bandage from his eyes and gazed out.

'Do you see her, Sharp-Eyes?' asked the Prince after a while.

There was no answer. The Prince waited anxiously, then at last Sharp Eyes said:

'Now I see her. Two hundred miles from here is a mountain. In the mountain is a rock in which is a precious stone, and that stone is her. When Long takes me there, we shall soon get her.'

Long immediately placed Sharp Eyes on his shoulders, stretched himself and strode off, covering twenty miles with every step that he took. As they approached the mountain, Sharp Eyes fixed his unbandaged gaze on it; the mountain crumbled, the rock split and shivered into a million pieces, and, reaching down, Long picked up the precious stone and turned and strode back to the Iron Castle clasping it securely.

For a moment the Prince held the jewel in his hand, then he tilted his palm and let the stone fall to the ground. As it touched the floor, it vanished and there stood the girl, as lovely, but also as pale and sad as ever. The next moment there was a bang as the door was flung open and in walked the wicked sorcerer. Seeing the girl standing in the middle of the floor, he made a nasty noise like a snarl and seized her by the hand. As he did so, there was a loud snap and a second iron hoop fell from his waist on to the floor. The old man muttered under his breath and dragged the girl out of the room, whereupon the door shut itself.

The Prince and his three strange servants spent another day exploring this extraordinary castle, where nothing stirred, and the grounds and gardens, where nothing grew, no bird sang or butterfly danced in the sunlight. It was a weird, uncanny place and the Prince was glad that they had only one more night to spend there – unless they failed to get the girl back, when they too would be turned to stone and remain there for ever.

That night after dinner, the sorcerer brought the girl in again, as before, and after seating her in a chair stalked out again, giving the Prince a very nasty look as he went. The Prince was determined to keep awake and decided that he would walk about. However, it wasn't long before his feet became leaden and his legs tired, so he sat down in the most uncomfortable chair and looked at Long, Broad and Sharp Eyes who were already stretched out, sound asleep. The Prince smiled and wished that there had been a more uncomfortable chair. Then he yawned and his eyes closed.

Suddenly the Prince woke with a start. I nearly fell asleep, he thought; then he saw that the window was grey and that it was nearly dawn and realised that he must have slept all night – and that the girl was gone. At once, he went and roused Sharp Eyes, who went to the window and after a while he called out:

'Three hundred miles from here is a black lake and in the middle of this, on the bottom, is a shell in which is a golden ring and that ring is the girl. Don't worry we'll get her, but it will take the three of us today.'

So Long set Sharp Eyes on one shoulder, Broad on the other; stretched himself to his utmost and strode off. With every step he covered thirty miles and in no time at all he had reached the black lake. There Sharp Eyes guided his hand as he reached for the shell, but long as his arm was, it was still not long enough to reach the bottom of the lake.

'Now you must help, Broad,' said Long. So Broad puffed himself out, then lying down, he began to drink. Before long he had drunk so much that the level of the water in the lake had sunk low enough for Long to be able to reach the shell. Taking the ring from it, he put Broad and Sharp Eyes back on his shoulders and set off back to the Iron Castle, but with Broad so full of water and heavy, he could not go quickly and his stride was shorter. Soon he realised that they would not get back in time, as he stopped to put Broad down. And all the time it was getting lighter and lighter.

Meanwhile, the poor Prince was standing at the window watching the pink of morning spreading up the sky and wondering desperately whether the three would get back in time before the door was flung open and the sorcerer came and saw that the girl was not there. The minutes passed. The first rays of the sun began to appear and the Prince trembled with apprehension. Then all at once he saw the rim of the sun appear above the horizon and heard the door being flung open. Turning, he saw the sorcerer standing in the doorway, a triumphant smile on his face. The sorcerer lifted his foot to step into the room and at that instant there was a crash and a tinkle as the window smashed, showering glass on to the floor, and there, in the middle of the room, stood the girl.

The sorcerer gave a bellow of rage. There was a loud crack and the third iron hoop fell from him and went rolling across the floor. Where the sorcerer had stood, there was now a raven, which gave a croak, flapped its wings and flew out through the broken window and away.

Turning to look at the girl again, the Prince saw colour flooding into her cheeks: then she smiled and, holding out her hand, came towards him. Then she began to speak, thanking him and his companions for setting her free and breaking the spell, and, as she spoke, there was a noise of stirring all over the castle. Those whom the wicked sorcerer had turned into stone came to life again. The door opened and people came running into the room to see who had set them free.

As they were all talking excitedly, Long and Sharp Eyes appeared and explained how, realising that they could not get back in time, Long had taken a great step forward and flung the ring through the window of the Prince's room, where it had landed on the floor just in time. The Prince explained to the people that it was really Long, Broad and Sharp Eyes they had to thank for saving them. They decided that they had had quite enough of the Iron Castle and set off in a great crowd to go to the Prince's home. Guided by Sharp Eyes they soon arrived and the old King wept with joy to see that his son had succeeded in his mission and returned home with the girl of his choice. There was a great feast and a huge wedding for the prince and the girl he had rescued.

Once all the excitement was over, Long, Broad and Sharp Eyes announced that they were going off to look for further adventures. The Prince tried to persuade them to stay with him, but they said that without feats to perform life was too dull and they must go and look for adventure, which is what they did.

FIVE

The Witch and the Horseshoes

LONG AGO in the mountains of Bohemia, there lived a rich, middle-aged farmer and his beautiful young wife. People wondered how they had met and married, for there was an air of mystery about her. She had long, black hair, a pale, oval face and her eyes were strange and had a far-away look. She did not make friends among her neighbours, she had no children and she seldom smiled, but for all this she made her husband a happy man and she cooked and kept his house neat and clean and did all the jobs that a good farmer's wife should do.

A young lad who looked after the sheep was very curious about the farmer's wife and even a little in love with her. He used to watch her and try to get her to laugh and joke with him, but she treated him with complete indifference.

One wild night – it was Hallowe'en, or All Souls' Night, the shepherd lad had to go out to an old ewe who was sick, and coming back past the farmhouse through the storm, he saw someone standing in front of the house. The moon broke free of the flying clouds and he saw with surprise that it was the farmer's wife. She lifted her arms to the moon, so the cloak she wore fell from her shoulders and in a voice as shrill as the wind she called out:

'Fly, fly!
Moon-high'

and at that moment she was whisked up in a gust of wind and vanished.

The shepherd boy was astonished and desperately curious, so he, too, stretched his arms to the moon and repeated the words,

'Fly, fly!
Moon-high.'

The wind roared louder and he was lifted up in a great strong gust and swept along through the darkness. Then he felt himself falling like a stone and he shut his eyes in terror. When he opened them all was still, the moon was shining brightly and he saw that he had come to the place where all the witches had their feast on Hallowe'en. There were wizened old hags, greasy, fat, gypsy-like creatures, and some who were younger, pale and slim with a strange beauty. In their midst sat his farmer's wife and her eyes met his and she recognised him. With a shriek she sprang up and turned herself into a black horse to escape, but before she could gallop away the shepherd lad leaped upon her back and, driven by a horror of the scene he had come upon, he rode the black horse without pity until they came to a blacksmith. There the shepherd asked him to shoe his horse, and though the horse kicked, the smith, who was a big strong man, shod well and strongly; then the shepherd rode the now quietened animal home.

Next day the farmer's wife limped as she walked and had seven little stab marks on each of her hands, in just the places where the nails come in a horseshoe. The marks never faded and she never told anyone how they had come, and the shepherd boy was too scared to tell, which meant confessing that once he had witnessed the witches' Feast.

SIX

Wolfgang

THERE WERE ONCE three young knights, who had fought in the Crusades and they were making their way home to Bohemia. In the fighting they had won plenty of money and jewels from their enemies, but two of the knights spent all their wealth on the way, drinking, gambling and leading a gay and extravagant life. The third, however, was a quieter, shyer young man and he still had the prize of gold and jewels that he had won from a rich Saracen.

The other two knights were jealous and wondered how they could rob Wolfgang of his wealth, but although he was quiet, he was no fool, and he kept his eyes open for treachery.

One day they arrived at the edge of a huge forest which stretched for many miles before them. After travelling through it for a whole day they still had not reached the other side, and they had to make camp in the forest for the night. They had shot a hare and were going to cook it for their supper. While they were away collecting wood for the fire, the two bad knights secretly made a plan to overpower Wolfgang that evening and take the bag in which he kept his jewels and gold. When they had made a good blaze and were seated round the fire, one of the knights heated a piece of iron and when it was red hot he and his companion fell upon Wolfgang. Blinding him with the iron, they took the bag with his gold and jewels and made off through the forest.

Poor Wolfgang was left blind and in great pain. He knew that it must be night-time, although he could not see, and in order to be safe from wolves or other wild animals that might be prowling, he crawled about until he found the trunk of a tree that he could climb and he managed to reach some branches, where he clung trembling and exhausted.

Soon the wind began to moan through the branches and other strange shrieks and unearthly noises came to Wolfgang's ears. It was Hallowe'en, and all the witches were on their way to their meeting-place in the mountains. Some flew over the forest, shrieking and calling to each other as they went, and others came down in the trees to rest, and chattered and muttered amongst themselves. Some of them perched in the branches near Wolfgang and he was terrified of their croaking voices and harsh screeches of laughter, but he listened, half-terrified, half-fascinated, to their strange talk.

Some of the witches boasted of their magic powers, while others argued that they were cleverer still and their shrill voices rose in dispute like a flock of noisy starlings. Some told horrible, cruel jokes and then they would all go off into fits of hideous laughter that made Wolfgang long to stop his ears against the dreadful things they were saying. Then, suddenly, he heard one begin to tell the story of his own misfortune. She described exactly how a knight had come to the forest and been attacked and robbed by his companions and

. . . he managed to reach some branches, where he clung trembling
and exhausted

she said that if the knight would bathe his eyes in the morning dew, his sight would be restored. Then she told how a town on the edge of the forest had been suffering from a terrible drought for three years, the people were dying of thirst and were in a desperate state, but if the knight went to the market-place, he would find there a statue, and if he dug beneath the statue he would find a spring of water. Thus he would save the town and earn himself a great reward and the gratitude of all the townspeople. She went on to say that if he travelled on to his home in Bohemia, he would find the Duke's daughter lying dangerously ill, with a terrible rash that no doctor could cure. She had been brought a magic fruit from a country far away which would cure her illness, but a bird had stolen it before the poor maiden could eat any of it, flown away and dropped it on the very top of the church tower. No one had seen where the bird had flown, and they were searching far and wide for the magic fruit. Then the witches began muttering and calling to each other, and suddenly they all rose up and flew away to their meeting-place.

Wolfgang wondered if he had been dreaming, or if he had really heard the witches talk, but in the morning, when he felt a gentle breeze stirring through the trees and heard the first birds begin to twitter and sing, he climbed stiffly down from the tree and felt the cool morning dew on the grass with his hands. He knelt down and, scarcely daring to hope, he carefully bathed his blind eyes with the fresh dew. Before long the burning pain in them ceased. He bathed them again and again, found that he could open his eyes and was overjoyed to find that he could see. Sunlight filtered through the tree-trunks which shaded the grass with a trellis pattern of twigs. The trunks were glowing with a pale green light, birds hopped and flew about the forest looking for their breakfasts and a few feet away from him a red squirrel sat up, nibbling a nut and watching him with shiny black eyes. For a moment Wolfgang held his breath in wonder, for nothing in his whole life had ever looked so beautiful before as that sunny autumn morning in the forest. Then he stood up, and the squirrel scrabbled up a tree-trunk and fled away through the branches.

After this, Wolfgang felt that all that the witch had said must be true. He journeyed on through the forest, until towards evening he came to the fringe of the trees and saw across the barren plain stretching away before him, the houses and towers of a town. A winding road led towards it, and Wolfgang set off at a brisk walk. He met several carts on his way that were loaded with tubs and barrels, but they were empty – the carters had been sent out to try and find water, but in this land of drought there was none to be had. He met other carts, too, carrying the bodies of people who had died of thirst.

As the sun went down Wolfgang came to an inn, and there he stopped for the night. During the evening he slipped out quietly to find the statue and he soon came to the market-place, which was quite deserted at that hour. In the middle of the cobbled square stood a statue of a knight and a dragon, and Wolfgang went cautiously up to it and tapped the stones at its base. One of them gave a hollow ring and Wolfgang went back to the inn full of excitement and hope.

In the morning he went to the mayor of the town

and asked him what reward he would get if he found water in the town. The mayor shrugged his shoulders and dismissed Wolfgang's question as not worth considering. But Wolfgang persisted and at last the mayor said:

'If you can find water in this town, you can have any reward. A hundred – a thousand – even ten thousand gold pieces.'

'Very well,' replied Wolfgang. 'If you will let me have two workmen with picks and shovels, I think I can soon put an end to your troubles.'

He took the workmen to the market-place and showed them the stone beside the statue and told them to dig. A little crowd collected to watch this strange sight and when the men levered up the stone, the earth beneath showed dark and damp. A little gasp went up from the people standing near and the two workmen went on digging with new hope. In a few more minutes a stream of water welled up and a spring went gushing and gurgling through the market-place. The people cheered and went mad with excitement. They rushed for buckets, jugs, mugs, anything in which to catch the precious water, while some knelt down by the spring and scooping up the water in their hands drank and drank.

Everyone came to thank Wolfgang and the mayor presented him with the ten thousand gold pieces. After staying a few days in the town, where everyone cheered and entertained him, Wolfgang said good-bye to the grateful townsfolk and continued on his way to Bohemia.

When he came to the city where he had been born, he noticed everyone had sad faces. He learned that the Duke's only daughter was now so ill that the doctors only expected her to live for a few more days. Wolfgang went to the Duke and pretended that he was a doctor who had come from a far-distant land to cure his daughter. The Duke, willing to try anything, agreed to let Wolfgang see the poor girl.

She was lying in her great bed, very small and pale, with the horrible rash that was yet unable to hide her great beauty. She was too ill to care who came to see her but she accepted a drink that the new young doctor had made for her and he promised to return in the morning.

That night, Wolfgang hurried to the churchyard and, summoning all his courage, he began to climb the tower, using only the rough stones and small niches and the thick growth of ivy on the tower for his feet and hand-holds. With a great effort he reached the top and found the magic fruit that the bird had dropped. Putting it in his pocket, he swung his leg over the edge, and began the dangerous climb down. He scrambled and slithered and hoped he wouldn't fall, but at last he reached the ground, scratched and breathless, but with a prize worth more than gold in his pocket.

The next morning he went again to visit the Duke's daughter and this time he coaxed her to eat the magic fruit. Then he sat beside her to watch the effect. She began to get better in front of his eyes and in a few hours the rash had quite disappeared. She looked at the young doctor sitting by her bed, and they smiled at each other.

The next day she ran to greet her father. She was completely cured and as lovely as ever. The Duke was so overjoyed to see his sweet daughter restored to health, that he promised Wolfgang half his lands as a reward and his daughter's hand in marriage, if he should wish it. Wolfgang was delighted, for he had fallen in love with the beautiful girl he had cured, and she loved him, too. So they were married and there were feasts and processions and great rejoicing in the city.

As Wolfgang now owned half the Duke's vast estates, he also had to help administer them, and one of his duties was to act as a judge in cases of law. One day a vagabond was brought before him. He had confessed to having been a crusader and on his way home, had robbed and blinded a young knight with the help of an evil companion. This companion had, in his turn, robbed the crusader whose friend he had pretended to be. Now the man was penniless and had been caught stealing turnips from a peasant's field. He was terrified when Wolfgang recognised him as one of the two bad knights who had attacked him, and knelt down and begged mercy. Wolfgang could only pity the man's poverty and wretchedness and be grateful for his own good fortune and happiness, so he pardoned the robber and allowed him to go free.

He was much loved for his kindness, and justice and he and his wife lived happily together.

SEVEN

The Woman of the Woods

BETUSKA WAS a little girl who lived in a tumbledown hut in the forest with her widowed mother. They were so poor that all they had to live on was the milk and cheese from two goats, some vegetables from a small patch of garden and a little money that they earned from the linen they could sell, which they made from flax grown in the meadow beside their hut.

Betuska used to spin the linen thread from the flax on her spindle while she looked after the goats, and her mother wove it into cloth when she was not busy working in the vegetable patch or the little cottage.

During the summer months, Betuska used to take the goats into the forest to graze in the various glades and clearings. She took with her a piece of bread for her dinner, the flax in a wallet and a distaff and spindle on which to wind the thread. Although she was poor and worked so hard and had no toys, no nice clothes and no friends but the two old goats, she was not an unhappy child. She was always merry and loved more than anything to sing and dance. As she drove the goats to their pasture she skipped and danced along the forest paths, then, while they grazed, she sat under a big tree and sang as she spun the flax into thread. At

midday Betuska would give a bit of bread to the goats
to keep them contented while she wandered off to pick
a few wild strawberries, or other berries that grew in
the woods to make her dinner of bread more appetising.
When she had finished her meal, she carefully brushed
the crumbs from her lap on to a flat stone, for the birds
to eat, and, while the goats lay on the sun-dappled
grass and chewed away, Betuska would dance in the
clearing until she was quite out of breath. Then she
would sit down and spin busily until the sun's rays
slanted low through the trees, which showed her it was
time to be on her way home. Driving the two goats
before her, she would return home with a full spindle
to her mother, who would hug her and tell her what a
good girl she was.

One day, when Betuska had finished her meal and
was about to dance on the grass, she suddenly saw a
beautiful girl standing in the clearing dressed in a
floating, filmy, white dress with a coronet of gold
gleaming on her shining golden hair. Betuska had
never seen anyone so lovely or so wonderfully dressed
and she stood there shyly, staring at this lovely vision,
while the old goats munched away and tugged at the
grass and bushes.

'Betuska, let us dance together!' said the prettiest
voice imaginable and the girl held out her arms as a
burst of glorious music sounded over their heads. In all
the trees sat a mass of birds, blackbirds, thrushes,
nightingales, goldfinches and chaffinches, singing and
singing for joy. Who could resist such an invitation?
Certainly not Betuska, whose greatest happiness was to
dance and sing. She skipped towards the beautiful
maiden and together their feet twinkled and flew, so

Betuska would dance in the clearing until she was quite out of
breath

lightly and so joyfully that they scarcely touched the ground. The strange thing was that Betuska danced and danced, but never grew tired, and by evening when the trunks of the big forest trees glowed redly in the setting sun, she was still dancing tirelessly until the music died away and suddenly she saw that the lovely, white-robed maiden was no longer there.

There was a coolness and silence in the still evening air and Betuska jumped when one of the goats trod, with a crackle, on a dry twig. Then she looked at her distaff and spindle lying neglected beside the flax and her heart sank when she realised that she had hardly spun any thread at all. She walked home feeling terribly ashamed of herself. If the lovely girl should come again to the clearing, Betuska was determined to refuse her invitation to dance and to work twice as hard to make up for her laziness. She was too upset to sing on the way home and the old goats kept glancing round at her, wondering what was the matter. Her mother, too, was surprised to have a quiet little girl coming home and asked if she felt ill. But Betuska said her throat was dry from singing so much and she hurried off to put away the flax hoping her mother was not going to wind off the thread until the next day when she could make up for lost time.

The next morning Betuska set off early, the sky was clear after a shower of rain and the drops on all the grass and leaves sparkled in the sun. She sang as she walked behind the goats. Their little hooves pattered on the path, the birds chirped and trilled and Betuska was eager to begin her spinning.

When they reached the clearing, she settled herself under the big tree and spent the morning spinning busily, while she sang softly to herself. At noon she stopped to give the goats the bit of bread they knew to expect, then she picked a big handful of wild strawberries for herself. When she had brushed the crumbs from her lap for the birds, she said, 'I cannot dance today, dear old goats,' and with a little sigh took up her spindle.

A small swish made her glance up and there before her stood the beautiful maiden, her blue eyes sparkling with fun. 'And why cannot you dance, my little shepherdess?' she asked.

'I dare not; forgive me,' replied Betuska, 'for I must fill my spindle before the sun sets, or my mother will be cross with me for doing so little yesterday.'

The lovely girl laughed and, high in the trees, a bird's trill echoed it. 'Come – dance! Dance with me now and I will help you finish your spinning before the sun sets.' She held out her hands, her mouth curved in a merry smile, the birds gathered in the trees above and their throats spilled out the loveliest music. Poor Betuska! Her feet itched to dance, she could not resist. She and the maiden stepped into the middle of the glade and their dancing was more perfect and joyful than before. As the sky filled with the colours of sunset, the bird song died away and a little breeze stirred in the glade. Suddenly Betuska could hear the old goats rustling about and her eyes fell on the flax and half-empty spindle. She burst into tears. The lovely maiden took the spindle and distaff and began to spin so fast that her fingers flew. Before the sun sank behind the trees all the thread was spun and she gave the full spindle to Betuska, looked at her with eyes grown cold in the evening light and suddenly she vanished.

That evening Betuska sang all the way home, as she drove the goats ahead of her. She thought the lovely stranger was so kind that if she came again she would dance with her and ask her name, so that she could tell her mother about her.

The next day she spent the morning spinning, but was hardly able to wait for the afternoon in case the maiden should come again. At noon she shared her bread with the goats and when they had finished, she rose and stretched her arms wide, 'Watch me, goats!' she laughed. 'I shall show you how I can remember my new dancing steps!' A sunbeam fell across her face and there was the lovely stranger in her shimmering dress and golden hair, standing before her. 'We will dance together,' she said, and once again the birds appeared and filled the glade with a flood of song. That afternoon the two girls danced more wildly and wonderfully than ever, Betuska felt as if she was as swift and strong as the wind, but when, at last, the stranger paused and the birds fell silent, it was already nearly dark and Betuska's eyes filled with tears when she saw the half-empty spindle.

'Give me your wallet,' said the stranger, 'I will make up for the time you have lost today.' Betuska did so, but the light was by now so dim beneath the trees that she could not see what the maiden put in the wallet, which she handed back with a warning. 'Do not look inside yet, but wait until you get home.'

Then there was no one in the glade, but the two sleepy old goats and Betuska herself.

She hurried off along the path and when she was out of the trees and the light was a little better, she could not resist peeping inside the wallet. It felt so light – as if nothing was inside it at all. Imagine poor Betuska's dismay, when she found only a wad of birch leaves in the wallet. 'Oh, I have been tricked!' she sobbed and angrily shook out the leaves. She was ashamed and unhappy and very afraid of what her mother would say.

Her mother was waiting for her outside the hut. 'Child, how late you are!' she said, 'and whatever sort of thread did you spin yesterday?'

'Why, mother?' asked Betuska.

'Because,' the widow replied, 'when I started to wind it, I wound and wound and still the spindle remained just as full as ever. At last I said, "this thread must be bewitched" and at that it vanished – spindle, distaff and thread – in a puff of smoke. What have you been doing in the forest, Betuska?'

Then the little girl told her mother the whole story, she described the lovely stranger and how they danced together, how she had spun the thread on the second day to make up for the first and how that evening she had promised a reward, but instead had only filled the wallet with leaves.

'My poor child! It was the woman of the woods!' cried the widow. 'Praise heaven that you are a girl, for little boys are crushed in the arms of the woman of the woods, or tickled to death; but sometimes, if she takes a fancy to little girls, she will treat them well and even pay them a rich reward. Let me look in that wallet, Betuska!'

They looked inside the wallet and there, in the corners – where Betuska had not shaken out all the leaves – lay some gold coins.

'It's lucky you didn't empty out all the leaves, but

in the morning you must take me to the place where you shook out the wallet and we will look for the rest,' said Betuska's mother.

In the morning, in the first light, they did go back along the path towards the forest, but when they came to the place where Betuska had taken her first peep. there was nothing but a little heap of withered leaves lying on the path.

Even so, the few gold coins brought them luck.

With them they bought more land and some cattle. Everything they did prospered, and soon they were able to buy a big farm and employ men to work on it, while they themselves lived comfortably and wore fine clothes.

Betuska never had to look after goats, or spin flax again, but she always loved dancing better than anything else. Sometimes at noon she would feel such a longing to dance again with the lovely stranger that she would secretly go back to the glade in the forest and wait – half-hopefully, half-fearfully – in case the maiden should appear again. But she never did.

EIGHT

The Child that Vanished

A CERTAIN NOBLE LORD, who lived in a great castle in one of the loveliest valleys to be found in the great mountains of Bohemia, had a strange dream just before his only son was born. He dreamed that the child must not touch the ground until he was ten years old or else something dreadful would happen. So, the noble lord, who was rather superstitious, engaged lots of nurses and gave orders that the baby was never to be allowed to touch the floor or the ground.

The baby grew into a child, but always, in accordance with its father's orders, it was either carried or wheeled about, never, never were its feet allowed to touch the ground. Then, one day just before the boy's tenth birthday, there was a tremendous commotion in the courtyard and the nurse who was carrying the child – a strapping, young country girl who had only had the job for a week – put the boy down and ran to the window to see what was going on. Almost at once, she remembered her orders and, turning round, saw to her horror that the boy was no longer where she had put him – nor was he anywhere in the room. Terrified, the girl ran to confess what she had done, and a great search was organised. The castle was searched from cellar to attic – not forgetting the roof – and the grounds and surrounding country combed, but there was no sign or trace of the boy anywhere.

Some time later, the chamberlain told the noble lord that strange things were happening in one of the big rooms in the castle; every night at midnight you could hear someone walking about there, groaning and lamenting. Something told the noble lord that here, perhaps, was a clue to the mystery of his son's disappearance, so he announced that he would give three hundred golden ducats to anyone who would spend the night in the room, so as to see what was happening. Over the years, lots of people tried, but the atmosphere in the room was so strange and uncanny that no one had the courage to stay there even until midnight, when the groans and footsteps started, and the poor father really lost hope of ever seeing his child again.

Not far from the castle, lived a widow who had two daughters. They were very poor and felt that three hundred golden ducats would be more than welcome, but they never dared offer their services, till they heard that other people had stopped trying. Then, the elder girl went to the castle and told the noble lord that she was willing to spend the night in the room. The noble lord warned her that anything might happen to her, but she said that they were so poor and had nothing to lose so she did not mind.

The girl was taken to the room, and told she could have anything she wanted, so she asked for this and that to cook for her supper, pots, cutlery and all she might need; then she asked for some logs and kindled a big fire in the grate, and sent for a bed. It took quite some time before she had got everything arranged to her liking and she was surprised to hear the clock strike twelve just as she was cooking her supper. When the twelfth stroke was still ringing in her ears, she heard the sound of footsteps and someone groaning quite close to her. Rather frightened. she looked into all the corners, but could see no one. Then, all at once, she saw a youth coming towards her:

'Who are you cooking for?' he asked the girl.

'Just for myself,' she replied pertly.

A faint expression of disappointment came over the youth's face. He looked sadly at the girl and asked:

'And for whom is the table laid?'

'Just for me,' the girl replied.

Again the youth looked disappointed.

'And this bed,' he said. 'Who is that prepared for?'

'Just for me,' said the girl.

Hearing this, the young man heaved a great sigh and disappeared.

In the morning the girl told the noble lord all that had happened, though without saying how disappointed the youth had seemed at her replies, or how unsympathetic she had been. She was given her three hundred ducats and went home well satisfied with herself.

The next week, the widow herself went to the castle and offered her services. Exactly the same things happened: the youth appeared as before, asked her the same questions and she gave the same answers, and again the disappointed youth sighed heavily and disappeared. In the morning, the widow told her story and received her reward, but the poor father was still no wiser and no nearer finding his son.

Some days later, the widow's younger daughter went

to the castle and offered her services to the poor father, who agreed to let her try, but felt rather sorry for her, as she looked such a nice, kind girl, and he was afraid something might happen to her. She, too, asked for pots and pans and all the ingredients for a nice supper and, going into the big room, she lit a good fire and made up the bed and laid the table and began cooking supper, feeling rather apprehensive about what might await her.

Before very long she heard the castle clock give the rumble it always gave before it struck and then: one, two, three, four, five, six, seven, eight, nine, ten, eleven – midnight was striking. As the twelfth stroke still vibrated in the air, she heard footsteps in the room and someone sighing and groaning. She could not see anyone, but when silence fell once more and she looked round again, she saw a youth coming towards her.

'Who are you cooking for?' the young man asked in a very pleasant voice.

The young girl was so moved by the sad expression on the youth's face and thought he looked so nice and kind, that she decided she was not going to be as rude as her sister and mother had been.

Again the young man asked:

'Who are you cooking for?'

Feeling somewhat embarrassed and awkward, the girl replied:

'I was cooking for myself, but if you would like some too, then for you as well.'

The youth's face lit up. Then he asked:

'And who did you lay the table for?'

'For myself,' said the girl, 'but if you will sit with me, then for you as well.'

A slight smile appeared on the young man's face. 'And the bed. Who is that for?'

'It was for me, but you can have it, if you would like.'

The youth beamed and clapped his hands.

'Thank you, thank you,' he said. 'I accept your invitation with pleasure. Will you, please, just wait a moment, while I go and thank my benefactors? Please wait, I shan't be long.'

The next moment, a great hole appeared in the middle of the floor through which a gust of warm spring air, heavy with the scent of flowers, swept into the room. Slowly, the young man descended into the gaping hole. Surprised – and somewhat frightened, but also very eager to know all that was going on, the young girl followed. Reaching the bottom of the chasm she found a whole new world stretched out before her. There was a river that looked like liquid gold, mountains with golden peaks and everywhere green meadows studded with flowers. Across these the young man walked, fondling each flower he came to, and soon they reached a wood, in which the trees were of solid gold. The moment they entered it, a flock of birds of all kinds came flying round the young man, twittering joyfully, alighting on his head and shoulders, and the young man, spoke to them and seemed to know them all. The young girl broke a twig off one of the trees and shoved it into her pocket as a souvenir.

Leaving this wood of golden trees, they walked across another small meadow and came to a second wood, in which the trees were all of silver. Entering it, the young man was at once surrounded by all sorts of animals, to which he spoke, patting and stroking them,

. . . a flock of birds of all kinds came flying round the young
man . . .

while they fawned and tried to get near him. While he stood there among them, the girl broke off a twig from one of the silver trees and put it in her pocket as a souvenir and proof of the marvels she was witnessing. She hoped that she was not doing wrong and that nobody would mind.

When the young man had thus said good-bye to all his friends, he turned and walked back the way he had come, followed by the girl. When they reached the place where the hole in the floor gaped above them, the girl took hold of the young man's coat-tails and was drawn up with him by some invisible force into the room. At once the hole in the floor closed and you could not see where it had been.

The fire was burning brightly and a delicious smell coming from the girl's cooking-pots.

'Well, I've said good-bye, so now let's have supper,' said the young man, and the girl quickly dished up.

They ate sitting side by side at the table. When they had finished, the young man yawned and said:

'I'm dreadfully sleepy. Let's go to bed.' Then he lay down on the bed and the moment his head touched the pillow, was sound asleep.

The young girl cleared the table and tidied everything away, then she too lay down and fell fast asleep.

The two slept on into the morning, so long that the youth's father, impatient to learn if the girl had been any more successful than her sister and mother, went himself to the room to hear her story. Entering, he could scarcely believe his eyes, when he saw his son lying there asleep. At that moment, the two sleepers awoke.

The noble lord shouted for his servants and officers

to come and see, and everyone was overjoyed that their lord's son had been found at last, rescued by the kind and generous nature of a young girl.

What was just as wonderful, was that the young man fell in love with his rescuer and married her, and they lived very happily together for years and years.

NINE

The Dancing Shoes

ONCE THERE WAS a youth named Jan, who was such a sleepyhead that he was always falling asleep in the most unexpected places and at the most inconvenient times. One day he was walking along the road and came to where a wagon was standing outside an inn. The bottom of the wagon was covered with hay and looked so warm and comfy, that Jan hopped in, stretched himself out and fell fast asleep.

When he had finished his lunch, the farmer came out of the inn, took off his horse's nosebag and drove on his way, never noticing Jan lying asleep in the hay. Later, turning round to get something he saw Jan, still asleep, and calling 'Whoa' to his horse, stopped and got down to investigate. At first, he did not know what to do, then, seeing an empty barrel standing by the wayside, he tipped sleeping Jan head-first into it and drove off, leaving him there, still asleep.

Jan slept on for quite a while and when he did wake up, of course had no idea where he was or how he had got into a barrel. He could hear a great pattering of feet and peeping out through the bung-hole, saw a lot of wolves, who had been attracted by the smell of human, circling round and round. They crowded

against the barrel, hairy sides brushing it, and the tip
of one's tail even came in through the bung-hole. Jan
seized it and pulling more of the tail inside took firm
hold. The wolf, frightened, tried to run away, but of
course the barrel followed it. The other wolves, seeing a
barrel chasing one of them, took fright and ran off
howling.

The terrified wolf ran and ran, the barrel bounding
behind it; then the barrel struck a rock and was
smashed. Jan let go his grip of the tail and the wolf,
freed, sped off into the darkness.

Jan discovered that he was in a wild part of the
mountains, he did not quite know where. As he walked
along rather aimlessly, turning a corner, he came
across a hermit. Hearing his story, the hermit said
that Jan might stay with him. 'In fact,' he added, 'I
am very glad that you have come, because I am going
to die in three days and would like someone to bury
me. If you will stay and do that I will reward you
handsomely.' Jan promised that he would.

So Jan stayed with the hermit. When the hermit
felt that he was about to die, he gave Jan a rod, a knapsack and a cap and said to him: 'In whatever direction
you point that rod and wish to be in a place there,
you will find yourself in it. Anything you want, you
will find in this knapsack and you have only to put on
this cap to make yourself invisible.'

The hermit then died and Jan buried him as he had
promised. Afterwards he sat down wondering what he
should do now. Feeling suddenly hungry, he thought
to himself how much he would like a roast chicken and
salad. Then he had an idea. Smiling to himself, he
undid the knapsack the hermit had given him and

looked inside. And, yes, there it was: a fragrant roast chicken and a fine crisp salad.

Having satisfied his hunger and licked his fingers, Jan thought he would try out his rod. So he pointed it in the direction in which he thought the King's palace to lie, and said: 'I want to be where the King is.'

The next moment, he found himself standing behind the throne in which sat the King in earnest conversation with his councillors. Appalled, Jan clapped the hermit's cap on his head and stood there as quiet as a mouse. Of course, he overheard everything that was said and so discovered that the Queen the King had recently married was either under a spell or herself an evil spirit from the underworld. Every night the Queen vanished, no one knew where or when, only that in the morning, twelve pairs of her dancing-shoes had been worn through. For days they had been trying to trace where she went, but so far no one had even seen her go. Now, they were going to offer a reward to anyone who could solve the mystery.

Hearing this, Jan thought he would have a try, so, sweeping off his cap, he suddenly presented himself in his crumpled rustic clothes and said he would like to try and find where the Queen went. The King asked who he was, and he said he was Sleepy Jan. The King said that he had heard of him and how did he think he was going to track the Queen, when he spent most of his time asleep. Anyway, Jan said he would like to try, and so it was arranged. That night, after the Queen had gone to bed, Sleepy Jan went to bed in the anteroom, through which she would have to pass, if she left her own room.

Strangely enough, Jan was able to keep awake. Soon he heard the Queen's door open and shut his eyes, pretending to be asleep. The Queen was carrying a candle and, to make sure that Jan was asleep, she ran the flame across the soles of his feet which were sticking out. Jan did not stir, or make a sound. Then the Queen picked up her twelve pairs of shoes and walked out.

The moment she had gone, Jan jumped out of bed, put on the hermit's cap and pointing his rod, said:

'I wish to be where the Queen is.'

At once he found himself near a great rock in front of which the Queen was standing, clutching her bag of shoes. Suddenly, the earth opened before her and two dragons emerged. She mounted one and, turning, they slid back into the earth. After a while Jan said again: 'I want to be where the Queen is!' and almost at once he found himself close behind the dragons in a forest where all the trees were made of lead. He broke off a twig and put it in his knapsack. As it broke, the twig gave off a ringing bell-like sound. The Queen heard it and felt afraid, but she rode on.

After a while, Jan again pointed the rod and found himself in another forest, where the trees were all made of tin. Again he broke off a twig with a ringing sound, which made the Queen turn pale, but she rode on. Jan waited a short while, then he used his rod again and found himself in a forest of silver trees. Again he broke off a twig and put it in his knapsack. When the Queen heard the ringing sound a third time, she fainted; but the dragons only hurried on.

By this time they reached a green meadow, the Queen had now recovered, and here she dismounted. All sorts of imps and ogres and spirits came crowding

round and a great feast was prepared, while Sleepy
Jan watched, invisible in his cap. One of the imps had
not arrived and his food was put aside for him, and
Jan gobbled it up, to everybody's considerable surprise.

Then music began to play and the Queen stood up
and began dancing with the imps and ogres. On and
on she danced, till she had worn through all her twelve
pairs of shoes; then she mounted one of the dragons
and the two of them took her back to the place where
the earth still stood open. By the time she had dismounted, Jan had used his rod and was there too.
Then he hurried ahead of her back to the parlour,
jumped into bed and pretended to be asleep. The
Queen looked at him closely as she passed, but seemed
satisfied that he really was asleep.

In the morning, the King's councillors told him that
none of them had managed to discover where the
Queen went, so they sent for Jan. They had great
difficulty in rousing him and he appeared all bleary-
eyed and yawning his head off. The King asked him
if he had seen the Queen leave her room.

'Yes, Your Majesty, I did,' he said.

'And did you follow her?'

'Yes, Your Majesty.'

'And see where she went?'

'Yes, Your Majesty.'

Then Sleepy Jan told him his story: how the Queen
had scorched the soles of his feet, how the earth had
opened before her beside a great rock and two dragons
had come and carried her to the lead forest – and here
he dived into his knapsack and produced a lead twig –
and then to the tin forest and the silver forest, again

On and on she danced, till she had worn through all her twelve
pairs of shoes

producing the tin and silver twigs he had broken off to prove his story; then he told about the feast and how the Queen had danced and finally been taken back to earth.

Then the King sent for the Queen and showed her the three twigs from the underworld that Sleepy Jan had brought back and, seeing that all had been discovered, the Queen gave a great cry, there was a clap of thunder and – the Queen was no longer there. She had, in fact, vanished and was never seen again, much to everybody's relief. The King especially was delighted and offered Sleepy Jan a rich reward, but what with his knapsack and his rod and his cap, Jan had everything he wanted, so, thanking the King, he set off once more in search of – sleep and adventure.

TEN

Count Horimir

IN THE DAYS of Duke Krzesomisl, long, long ago, Bohemia was rich in precious metals and its rivers carried grains of gold with them from the distant mountains. The Duke, however, was not content with gold that his people got for him by collecting these grains, but ordered them to burrow into the mountains through which these rivers ran in order to get him more, much more. So they burrowed into and under the mountains, making long shafts and galleries and getting much gold and silver for their Duke, who paid them handsomely, so handsomely that most young men wanted to be miners instead of working on the land and before long you could see fields that had not been tilled, because there had been no one to till them, and wolves and bears killed many of the farmers' sheep, because there was no one to look after them.

Food became scarce in the rich land of Bohemia, and then came disaster: for forty weeks the sky remained cloudless and no rain fell. Not a drop. Seed that had been sown did not sprout, grass did not grow, trees did not blossom and the rivers dried up. Then people became frightened and hungry and went in crowds to the Duke and asked for food for themselves and their children, and also, that he should recall the people from the mines so that, when the drought ended – if it ever did – they would be able to till all the fields and sow the corn they needed to prevent people going hungry. The Duke listened to what they had to say and promised to do something; but when everyone had gone back home again, he thought to himself that even if food was short, he himself would never lack and there would always be enough for his miners, so that he would rather have his gold and silver as before, and as a result he did nothing.

His people, of course, expected him to do as he had promised and that the men would soon leave the mines in the mountains and come back to their homes. This expectation was shared by Count Horimir, a noble man who cared well for his people and was one of the greedy Duke's councillors. Again and again Count Horimir went to the Duke, telling him that he must close the mines in order to save the people.

Now, the miners did not want to leave the mines and go back to working on the land, where, instead of big wages, they would get just the same as everyone else, and they hated Count Horimir for giving the Duke this advice and decided to try and kill him. They made a plan, and then a large number of them set off by night intending to reach the Count's castle at dawn and surprise him in bed. But Count Horimir had the gift of reading the stars and these warned him to keep a look out, with the result that he saw the miners from the top of his castle tower while they were still a long way off. Realising their evil purpose, he left his castle and went to complain to the Duke.

When the miners reached the castle and found that the Count had escaped them, they were furious and went to his barns and store-rooms pulling out all the corn and food they found there which they spitefully burned and destroyed. They hoped that the Count who had talked so much about people starving, should now go hungry himself.

The Duke gave the Count a friendly reception and promised to punish the miners, but in his heart of hearts he had no intention of doing anything of the kind, because he thought more of his miners than of anyone else and he only gave the promise in order to pacify the Count. Count Horimir realised that this was so, and he was very sad and felt sorry indeed for the people of his country.

At the end of a long day which the Count had spent walking about noting the sufferings of the people and wondering what could be done to make their lot lighter, he found himself at the foot of a great cliff. Suddenly, he saw an old man standing there holding a wonderful grey horse by the bridle. The man was tall and dressed in a long white robe; he had a beard that reached to his waist and his bearing was kingly and dignified.

'Take this noble animal,' he said. 'Its name is Schennick and if ever you are in danger or great difficulty, call it by name and it will help you. First, however, you must go with it and block up all the entrances to the mines, because as long as they remain open, the people of this country will go hungry.'

Saying that, the old man put the reins into Count Horimir's hand; then a great cleft appeared in the cliff behind him, he stepped back into it and the rock

... Count Horimir found himself flying with it through the air ...

closed again. It was as though he had never been there. But the horse remained to show that it had not been a dream. It whinnied and pawed at the ground with its hoof, as though reminding Horimir that they must hurry. The Count put up his hand and patted its arching neck and spoke to it in a low, loving voice:

'Schennick, dear Schennick, I have need of your help.'

Then he swung himself into the saddle, the horse gave a bound and Count Horimir found himself flying with it through the air, rushing with the speed of the wind towards the gold and silver mines. Whenever they came to a mine, they dropped to the ground and Schennick kicked at the mountain making great masses of rock and earth fall into the shafts and galleries, till they were completely blocked. A great full moon watched them as they went thus from mine to mine, and by midnight they had finished. Then Schennick leaped into the air again and took the Count back to the Duke's castle faster than the wind could have carried him. The Count went to bed, and at dawn the next morning he was as usual at the Duke's bedside, waiting to serve him.

Three days later the reports and complaints began to come in, and they all said that this was the foul work of Count Horimir. The Duke was furious and swore to punish the Count and ordered his arrest. The other councillors and the Count's friends reminded the Duke that each morning Horimir had stood at his bedside to receive his orders, so he could not possibly have been to the mines all those many miles away. And anyway how could one man, or even a few men, have moved all the mass of rock and earth that now blocked the mines? It was not humanly possible. But the Duke would not listen. He was too angry and also his conscience pricked him, because the Count had so often reminded him of his promise to recall the miners, which he had never intended to do. So the Duke set up a court to try Count Horimir and the judges, afraid of the Duke's anger, passed sentence of death, which, they knew, was what the Duke wanted.

So they built a scaffold in the great courtyard of the castle and made all preparations for the execution. When the dread day dawned, Horimir suddenly remembered what the strange kingly figure had said about Schennick, and his heart lightened with hope. Then he sent a message and asked if he might speak to the Duke, and the Duke let him come to him. Then the Count asked, as a favour, that he might be allowed one last ride round the great courtyard on his noble horse that had so long been his friend and companion. The Duke smiled, because he thought this was a very transparent little trick, but he said that the Count could have his ride *after* all the gates had been shut and barred. So, as soon as the great gates were shut, the Count was allowed to go to the stables and saddle his horse for a last ride.

Schennick looked round and whinnied when it saw the Count, and the Count patted its neck and stroked its velvety muzzle and whispered so that none of the guards could hear:

'Schennick, dear Schennick, I have need of your help.'

Then he led Schennick out into the great courtyard

and swung himself into the saddle. Schennick took a step or two forward, then leaped into the air and on and away over the castle wall, across the plain and the waters of the Moldav, until they came to Count Horimir's own castle, and there Schennick dropped down and stopped beside the gate. The Count's people came running up, faces alight with surprise and happiness. They crowded round the great horse, praising it and wanting to pat it and thank it for saving their master. They made a hot bran mash and brought sugar and apples and all the things horses are most fond of, but Schennick would eat none of it. The next morning they found him standing in his loose box with drooping head, looking forlorn and ill. The Count came hurrying into the stable, and, to his astonishment, heard Schennick speak:

'If I stay here, I must die,' the horse said. 'Will you not, in return for my help, take me back to the cliff, where you got me. I have done what I was meant to do and my hour is upon me.'

The Count was horrified to think that Schennick might feel him ungrateful and at once led him out of the stable, through the castle gate and on across the fields, till they were in sight of the cliff. As they approached, the rock split and the regal figure in the long white robe appeared again. Schennick's head went up, he pricked his ears and whinnied.

'Thank you, Count, for bringing Schennick back to me,' said the man. 'Many long years ago I was Duke of Bohemia and I could not see my people suffer. You have helped them and now all will be well. Thank you and farewell.'

The man took Schennick by the bridle and led him

slowly into the cleft, again the rock closed and was as if it had never opened.

Count Horimir turned and went slowly home. There he found a messenger from the Duke, who, of course, had been more than astonished at the Count's miraculous escape and, realising that he was dealing with a man with powers more than natural, had decided that he would rather have him as a friend than an enemy. So, the messenger said, the Duke asked the Count to forgive his unfairness and to return to the Castle to help him govern his dominions. If he would do this, the Duke promised to take his advice in all things.

And because Count Horimir was both good and wise, and above all because he wanted to help the people of his fair country, he forgave the Duke and worked with him and for him for many years.

ELEVEN

The Yezinkas

THERE WAS ONCE a poor boy whose father and mother were both dead. There was no one to look after him, so he had to go out into the world to find some work which would at least earn him food and shelter.

He walked a long way without finding anyone who was willing to employ him and at last he came to a little farmhouse, standing all by itself in a wood. Sitting in the sunshine in the doorway was an old man who was blind, and in a pen near by some hungry goats were bleating. 'My poor goats, I would gladly take you to the pasture, but I cannot see and I have no one to send with you,' he said.

'Oh, please let me lead the goats for you,' begged the boy. 'I have nothing to do, no home and no family and I would gladly stay and help you.'

'Who are you?' asked the old man.

'My name is Josef,' replied the boy, 'and I will stay with you and work for you as long as you like.'

'Good boy!' said the old man delightedly, 'you are the answer to my prayers. Now lead the goats out to graze, but do not take them on to the hillock in the woods, or the Yezinkas will catch you, lull you to sleep and then tear your eyes out – which is what they did to me.'

'Don't worry, grandfather,' said Josef, 'I've been used to living on my wits, and the Yezinkas will not tear out *my* eyes.'

So Josef let out the hungry goats and for three days led them to different clearings and glades in the woods, where the short grass was sweet and watered by a little woodland stream. At night he prepared supper for himself and the old man and drew water from the well for the morning, then he went to sleep, happy to have found a home and a job so much to his liking.

On the morning of the fourth day Josef swept and tidied the little house as usual and left the old man some bread and cheese to eat during the day, then taking some for himself, he called to the goats and set off again into the woods. The goats pressed on ahead towards the hillock and Josef thought to himself – 'Why should I fear the Yezinkas? The grazing is good round the hillock and why shouldn't the goats have the best?' So saying he cut three thorny bramble stems and tucked them under his hat, then he drove the goats straight on towards the hillock. Reaching the smooth green mound of grass, he sat down on a boulder and watched the goats nibbling away greedily. Suddenly he looked up and saw a lovely girl standing beside him, she was dressed in white and had beautiful dark glossy hair tumbling over her shoulders and fine sparkling eyes, as black as midnight.

'Good morning, shepherd boy,' said the maiden. Would you like to try one of the apples from my garden? I promise they're the sweetest you will have

And she held out a rosy apple in her small hand

ever tasted!' And she held out a rosy apple in her small hand.

But our Josef was no fool. 'Aha!' he thought to himself, 'And if I was to eat that apple, my fine maiden, I know what would be my fate. I should fall asleep and then you would pluck out my eyes.'

'No thank you,' he said aloud, 'my master has apple-trees that grow fruit even more delicious than yours and I have eaten enough of them already!'

'If you do not want it, I shan't try and persuade you,' said the girl – and then she was gone.

A short while afterwards another lovely young girl appeared before Josef and she was even prettier and more appealing than the first.

'Greetings, shepherd boy!' she called gaily holding out a beautiful red rose in her hand, and she asked him to smell its fragrance. 'I have just picked it. Let me tuck it in your jacket, so you may enjoy its sweet scent, too,' she said.

'Thank you, my fair maiden,' said Josef, 'But my master has even more beautiful roses in his garden. And I have smelled them to my heart's content!'

'Oh well, if you don't want it,' said the girl crossly and she turned and slipped away.

Josef grinned a broad grin and sat down on the boulder again to watch his goats. Presently a third maiden appeared and she was even more beautiful and finely dressed than the other two.

'Good morning, my handsome shepherd,' she said in flattering tones, 'what a shame that you have no one to comb that bright hair of yours! Come, let me comb it tidily for you and you'll be the best-looking lad in the kingdom!'

And she stepped towards him with her hand outstretched. Josef took off his hat, pretending to let her comb his hair, but instead he whisked out one of the bramble stems and bound it quickly round the maiden's wrists. She began to struggle and cry for help and to weep and beg for mercy until the other two girls came running to the scene. When they saw what Josef had done to their sister they pleaded with him to set her free, but the sensible boy took no notice of their sweet entreaties and told them to set her free themselves.

'Oh, shepherd boy, our little hands are so soft and tender, we should tear them to bits,' cried the girls. But Josef was firm, and at last they went to the struggling girl and tried to set her free. This was just what Josef was waiting for, and with a swift movement, he whisked out the other two brambles and bound the wrists of the two girls as firmly as the first.

'Now I've got you, you wicked Yezinkas,' he said sternly, 'and you shall give back my master's eyes that you plucked from his head, or I shall throw you into the water!' The first girl pretended to know nothing, but Josef prepared to throw her into the stream, which flowed into a deep pool at the foot of the hillock, so she begged for mercy and promised to give him back the eyes if he would then let her go free.

She led him towards a cave in the hillside, the entrance to which was screened by brambles and overhanging ferns. Thrusting them aside, Josef entered and saw upon the floor of the cave a heap of human eyes, blue and brown and black and grey. He ordered the girl to pick up his old master's eyes and give them to him and then, driving the Yezinkas ahead of him, as if they were the goats, he returned to the little farm-house and called for his master. But when Josef fitted the eyes into the old man's head, he could see nothing and began to cry with disappointment.

Josef was undaunted. Angrily he drove the girls back to the hillock and he flung the first one, who had deceived him, into the deep pool. She sank under the dark water and was never seen again.

Then he turned to the other two and, threatening them with the same fate if they deceived him, ordered them into the cave to find his old master's eyes. Again one of the girls picked up a pair of eyes, again Josef returned with them to the old man and fitted them into his head, but 'Alas! Alas! These are not my eyes,' wailed the old man, 'for I can see nothing.'

With a shout of anger Josef drove the two frightened girls back to the hillock and hurled the second girl into the pool, when she sank below the surface.

There only remained the youngest Yezinka and to her Josef spoke in a hard voice saying she must find his master's eyes or be drowned in the pool with her sisters. Sobbing and protesting, she took him into the grim cave and picked out a pair of eyes from the heap. But she, too, was deceiving Josef, for when he gave the third pair of eyes to his master, the poor old man was as blind as ever.

'All right!' said Josef. 'Get back to your hillock and I shall delight in seeing you drown in that black water.' Then the last Yezinka knew that there was no hope for her, unless she gave back the real pair of eyes to the old man. She begged for one more chance and she went back to the cave and took a pair of eyes from the bottom of the heap.

Almost afraid to hope, Josef took the eyes back to his master and, when they were fitted into his head, the old man gave a glad shout.

'My son! God be praised! I can see perfectly,' cried the old man and he embraced Josef and together they danced with joy.

Then Josef removed the bramble fetters from the wrists of that lovely but deceitful Yezinka and told her to be off and never come near them again. Certainly, she was never seen or heard of again in those parts, but years later tales of strange happenings in a distant part of Bohemia made Josef wonder. But that is another story altogether.

With his sight restored, the old man and Josef lived very happily together. Josef looked after the goats and the old man made cheese from their milk and the beautiful, cruel Yezinkas were never seen again.

TWELVE

The Golden-Haired Princess

THERE WAS ONCE an old King who lived in a small, but rich kingdom in the part of Europe that we now call Czechoslovakia, but was once Bohemia. He had almost everything that anyone could wish for, but he was grumpy and discontented and for ever wanting something more.

One day an old countrywoman came to his palace with an eel in a basket. She brought it to the King and told him that if it was cooked, anyone who ate it would be able to understand the language of all the birds and animals and insects in the world. The old King was greatly pleased, for this offered him a wonderful opportunity to possess a gift no other mortal could possibly have, so he called his servant Jan, told him to give the old woman a purse of gold coins for the eel and to cook it for the King's dinner immediately. But on pain of death, he was not to eat so much as a morsel of the eel himself, and he was to serve it only to the King.

Jan thought this must be a very strange eel for his master to pay for it with a purse of gold and to give such strict instructions about it, so when it was cooked, out of curiosity he picked a tiny piece off the eel to

One day an old countrywoman came to his palace with an eel in
a basket

taste, and was puzzled to hear tiny voices by his ear saying 'Give us a bit! Give us a bit!' He could see nothing but some flies buzzing round the kitchen. Suddenly he realised the voices were coming from them – he knew that the eel was magic and this was the reason for his master's orders. He ate one more little piece, then carried the dish to the king, determined to let him know nothing of what he had done.

When the King had dined, he told Jan to order two horses to be saddled and that he wished them to go for a ride together.

After they had left the palace courtyard and struck off across the park, Jan's horse gave a buck and a snort and he heard it say to the other horse, 'I feel so fit, I could jump over a mountain!' The King's horse blew through its nostrils in reply, saying, 'So could I, but I can't frisk about, or this silly old fool would fall off and break his neck.' Jan's horse said, 'Serve him right if he did, then you might have someone a bit more lively on your back.' Jan nearly burst with laughter to hear the horses talking like this, but he bit his lip hard to stop the laughter and forgot that of course the old King had also understood what the horses were saying. The King glanced round at Jan, suspicious of his odd expression and asked, 'What are you sniggering about?' 'Nothing, your Majesty,' replied Jan. 'Hm,' grunted the King and turned his horse for home, he didn't trust the horses after hearing them talk. And he didn't trust Jan, either.

When they returned to the palace, the King ordered Jan to pour him out a goblet of wine, adding that if he let one drop spill over, he should have his head cut off. Poor Jan was much afraid and carefully began to pour the wine when two sparrows flew in at the window quarrelling shrilly. Jan and the King could understand their angry chirps – one was saying, 'Give me one of those golden hairs!' 'No – they're mine,' shrieked the other. 'I saw the golden-haired Princess combing them from her hair,' squeaked the first and with this tugged one of the hairs from the other sparrow's beak. At that moment they dropped a golden hair in their tustle and it fell to the ground with a little tinkle. Jan turned his head, and in doing so over-filled the goblet and some wine spilled on to the table. 'I could kill you for that,' growled the King, 'But I will spare your life if you bring me the Princess with this golden hair for my wife.'

Jan bowed and withdrew from the King's presence. He was in despair, for he had no idea how to begin to look for the unknown Princess. Thoughtfully, he ordered his horse to be saddled and rode out from the palace uncertain of which direction to take. He let his horse choose its own way and presently he found himself riding through a forest. He saw a fire burning which some woodcutters had lit by the path near a large ant-heap, and the heat and sparks had driven the ants from their nest. Jan heard them saying, 'Oh, who will help us? Our eggs are burning and we will be killed in the fire if we rescue them.' Their tiny voices were so pitiful that Jan jumped down from his horse and beat out the fire with a branch. The ants called in gratitude that if ever he needed their help he could count on them. Jan smiled at the idea of the little ants helping him and he mounted again and rode on. A little farther on, Jan came to a tall tree in which was a raven's nest. Two young ravens had fallen from the nest and were huddled together piping sadly. 'Oh, we are so hungry and we are too young to fly up to our nest.' Jan again dismounted and gently picking up the young ravens he put them in the bag that was slung round his shoulders, climbed the tall tree and carefully returned them to their parents on the nest. The ravens croaked thankfully to him, 'If ever you need our help, you have only to call and we will come.'

Once more Jan mounted his horse and rode on through the wood for a long way. At last the trees began to thin out and the track led down to the shores of a huge lake, which lay calm and glittering as far as the eye could see. Jan led his horse down to the water's edge to drink and came across two fishermen having a furious quarrel. They had caught a big golden fish in their net and were arguing as to which of them should keep it. One man said he had caught the fish, the other said it was his net, therefore his fish. All this time the fish flapped and gasped and Jan could understand the distress and anguish of its voice. So great was his pity for the fish that he offered to give the two fishermen all the money that he had in his purse, which they could divide equally, in return for the fish. The two men were delighted at this offer, for the fish wasn't worth all that money and they took it before he should change his mind. Jan lifted the fish from the net and placed it back in the shallows of the lake. Before it swam happily away, it leapt once from the water and called to him, 'In return for your kindness, I will help you whenever you need me.'

The fishermen were very surprised at Jan's odd behaviour, first to give all his money for the fish and then to let it go free. They asked him what he was

doing by the lake, and where he was going. Jan told
them about his master, the old King, who had ordered
him to search for a Princess with golden hair and bring
her back for his bride. 'But,' he added sorrowfully, 'I
am never likely to find her, for I have no idea where to
look for her.'

'She must be the golden-haired daughter of the King
who lives on the island in the middle of this lake!'
exclaimed the fishermen. 'Every morning at sunrise
she combs her golden hair and it sparkles and flashes
in the sun's rays. Look, you can just see the top of the
crystal tower which is on the castle, shining across the
water.'

'We can row you to the island in our boat in return
for settling our quarrel,' said one of the fishermen.
'But be careful to ask for the right Princess,' said the
other. 'The King has twelve daughters, but only one
of them has golden hair.'

Jan thanked them for this valuable information and
was soon rowed across to the island. There, he jumped
ashore and climbed a steep, winding path that led up
to the crystal castle. He asked to see the King and was
taken into a beautiful room where a gentle-faced old
man was playing chess with one of his courtiers. Jan
bowed and asked for the hand of the golden-haired
Princess for his master, the neighbouring King. The
old King smiled a strange smile, considered the game
of chess for a moment before replying, 'Yes, you shall
take her. But you must win her for your master.
Tomorrow you must perform a task that I shall set for
you. If you succeed in that, you must perform another
that I shall set the following day – and again another
on the third day. Meanwhile my servant shall take

you to a room where you can refresh yourself and rest.'

Jan was taken to a well-furnished room where a table was already laid with many good things to eat. He was hungry from his long day's travel and ate a good meal, then settled down to sleep.

Next morning he was wakened early and told to come before the King to be instructed in his first task. The King was seated by an open window and, pointing to a meadow which lay beyond the castle grounds, he told Jan that his golden-haired daughter had been walking in the meadow when the thread of her pearl necklace had broken and all the pearls had scattered in the long grass. 'You must collect them all, young man,' said the King, 'for even if one pearl is missing, you will have failed in your task.'

Jan went out to the meadow. He walked up and down and all round it, he knelt down and peered through the long grass, but not a single pearl could he see.

'Oh dear,' sighed Jan, 'here is something that my little ant friends could help with, if only they were here.'

'Here we are, kind friend,' came a little voice near Jan's knee. 'How can we help you? You have only to say.'

Jan saw the ground between the grasses was swarming with ants, so he told them of his difficult task and at once they scurried off. Soon they came back in twos and threes rolling the first of the pearls through the long grass to Jan's feet. Presently he had a handful of pearls and the ants told him that they could find no more. He thanked them warmly and was just turning to go back to the castle when he heard a tiny voice calling, 'Wait! Wait!' It was a little ant with a lame foot that had been burnt in the fire and it could not run as quickly as the others. It brought the last small pearl to Jan, then he tied them all up in his handkerchief, thanked the little ants again, and walked gaily back, his first task complete.

The King received him, counted the pearls and found none missing, so he told Jan that he had performed his task well and that tomorrow he would give him something else to do.

The next morning the King again sat by his open window and this time pointing to the shore of the island he said, 'The Princesses sometimes bathe in the lake and the other day my golden-haired daughter lost a golden ring while she was swimming. This you must find and bring to me.'

Jan walked down to the shore and looked into the water. The lake was beautifully clear, but the beach shelved so steeply that the water quickly became too deep for Jan to see the bottom.

'I wish my golden fish could help me,' said Jan aloud and in a moment there was a splash and a flash and the golden fish was swimming near him.

'What do you need?' asked the fish, 'for I will certainly help you.'

'The King has told me to find his daughter's golden ring, which she has lost in the lake,' said Jan, 'and without your help I shall never find it.'

'Aha,' said the fish, 'only just now I met a pike wearing a golden ring on his fin. Just wait a little and I will bring it to you.'

With a swirl the fish was gone and Jan was left with

the wavelets lapping at his feet, wondering if all these strange happenings were a dream. But in a few minutes the golden fish was back again carrying the golden ring in its mouth. Jan held his hand on the surface of the water and with a chuckle the fish spat the ring into his open hand. Jan's spirits rose at the successful outcome of his task, and he bounded up the steep path to the castle, went straight to the King and laid the ring on the table at his side.

The King congratulated Jan and told him to return the next morning for his final task.

In the morning early, Jan again went to the King who looked at him a little strangely as he said, 'Today you must bring both dead and living water for my golden-haired daughter, for if she is to be your master's bride, she will have need of it.'

This time poor Jan did not even know what he was looking for or where to look. He struck off into the centre of the island, where he had never been before, hoping that he might find a spring that perhaps could be the living water, but he found himself entering a dark wood, with no sound but the wind in the tree-tops above him. 'It is like the wood where I found the ravens,' thought Jan, 'perhaps being such wise birds, they could now help me.'

'Of course we can!' came a harsh croak just above Jan's head, which nearly made him jump out of his skin, and there on a low branch sat the two young ravens. 'What is it you need?' they asked.

'I have been told to bring dead and living water, but what it is and where it can be found, I just don't know,' said poor, puzzled Jan.

'We know,' croaked the ravens, 'just stay here a

while and we will return with it,' and they flew away
through the trees.

Jan waited a little and then he heard the rush of
wings and the two ravens settled at his feet carrying in
their beaks two nut-shells filled with water. 'This is the
dead water,' said one raven, 'And this the living,'
replied the other, then, after placing the precious
nut-shells carefully in Jan's hands, they hopped on to
a branch and flapped away. Jan called his thanks to
them and turned back towards the castle. He had not
gone far when he heard a small voice calling out for help
and saw a fly caught in a spider' web and struggling
frantically to free itself. The spider was advancing towards the fly and sank its jaws into its victim's body. The
struggles ceased as Jan approached. He flicked one drop
of the dead water on to the spider and it immediately
dropped to the ground like a stone. Then he sprinkled
the fly with living water and it stretched and scraped
its legs clear of the web and flew up into the air.

'It's a lucky thing for you, Jan, that you restored me
to life,' buzzed the fly, 'for without my help you could
never guess which of the King's daughters is the
golden-haired Princess.'

When the King saw that Jan had completed his
third task he said that he would give him his golden-
haired daughter, if he could pick her out from the
twelve Princesses.

The King led the way to a great hall in the centre of
which was a round table. Twelve beautiful girls sat
round the table and round each one's head was bound
a long white wimple which fell in folds to the ground
and covered up their hair completely, so that they all
looked alike.

'Here are my daughters,' said the King. 'Only one of them has golden hair and if you choose her, she is yours. But if you cannot find her the first time, then you will not have a second chance.'

Jan looked wonderingly round the table. The girls sat still, their hands in their laps, their eyes downcast. And they all looked so alike! Then he heard the little voice buzzing close to his ear. 'Walk round the table a little – not this one no, nor the next, nor yet the next – now, this one, this is the one!'

'Give me this Princess!' cried Jan, looking straight at the King and the old man nodded gravely and said, 'Yes, you have guessed right and have won her for your master.' He told his daughter to rise and take off her head covering and as she did so her beautiful hair shook free and flashed with such a golden fire that Jan's eyes were dazzled. Preparations were made for the journey and the following day Jan set out with the Princess and a fine escort provided by her father.

Late that evening the procession rode into the palace courtyard and when the old King heard the clatter of horses' hooves and the jingling of their harness, he peeped from a window above and rubbed his hands with delight to see the beauty of the golden-haired girl who sat very slim and straight on her horse and who was to be his bride. He bit his lip with sudden jealousy when he noticed the sweet smile on her face as Jan helped her down from her horse and he drew back from the window and sat hard-faced and bitter, waiting for the Princess to be brought before him.

Jan led her by the hand into the King's chamber and waited for a word of praise or recognition from his royal master. But none came. Instead the old King said, 'Tomorrow I shall wed the princess and, as you have succeeded in your task, I shall not have you beheaded and thrown to the ravens as I had intended!' He paused, 'I shall give you decent burial instead. You shall be executed in the morning before my wedding.'

Poor Jan was taken away by guards and although the Princess begged for his life to be spared, the old King was unmoved by her tears.

In the morning Jan was led out in front of the palace and, while frenzied preparations for the royal wedding went on, he was executed before the king. Then the Princess asked her master if she could have the dead servant's body and, her request being granted, she sprinkled his corpse with the living water from the nutshell, which her father had given her when she left his island. Immediately Jan stretched and stirred, yawned and sat up murmuring that he felt much refreshed from his good sleep. He looked younger, gayer and more handsome than ever before and the old King was amazed and angry, but it also gave him an idea. If the magic had made Jan more handsome, could it not do the same for him and make him feel younger too? So, he commanded the girl to sprinkle him with the magic water. What he did not know was that there was no more living water left, so the Princess took the other nut-shell in her hand and sprinkled it on the King's head instead. At once the King fell to the ground dead, and, after his display of ingratitude and cruelty no one could be sorry.

When they heard that the King was dead, the people asked that Jan – with his understanding of all living creatures and the Princess with her knowledge of magic should be their King and Queen instead. Being very much in love, they were married straight away, and Jan's animal friends came to offer their good wishes at the wedding. The sun shone on his beautiful golden-haired bride and they lived happily ever after.

THIRTEEN

The Giants of Scharka Valley

THE SHEPHERD, who looked after the sheep of the old Duke of Prague, was a kindly, gentle man, who lived alone with his son, Jaroslav, since his wife had died many years before. Jaroslav was born one winter's night and, on his first birthday, a wild and stormy night, the shepherd and his wife had heard a knock on the door of their cottage just as a great gust of wind had gone shrieking and rattling past. Opening the door they had found a pilgrim, who asked for shelter for the night. They gladly took him in and, while the wife was preparing a meal for him, the stranger went and stood by the cradle, looking down at the little boy, whose birthday it was. In the morning, before he left, the pilgrim gave the shepherd a golden zither and an ivory rod and told him to keep them for his son. If you played a merry tune on the zither, he said, it would make anyone dance and jump about, even against his will; if you played a soft, gentle melody on it, you would win the friendship and affection of whoever heard it. The ivory rod was very different: if you were in danger, being attacked by someone much stronger than yourself, you had only to touch him with its knob and he would fall down dead at your feet.

Thus, said the pilgrim, if the shepherd's son knew how to use those gifts sensibly and well, he would achieve high honours and perhaps even a kingdom.

This the shepherd repeated to his son, as, old and weary, he lay dying, but he took care to add that of course kingdoms were not for such as he and he must be content to live a modest decent life; then he asked the youth to play a merry tune on the zither and so died with a smile on his face.

The first thing the young man had to do was to go to Prague and ask the Duke if he might tend the ducal flocks in place of his father. Being so young, he was afraid that he might not be allowed to do so; but the Duke was gracious and said that he might be the ducal shepherd, but, he added, 'I must warn you of the dangers that threaten your flocks and you. Not far from the royal pastures, westwards of your cottage, is a narrow valley lying between cliffs and pleasant hills. Here, once upon a time, cunning Scharka captured Zeman Stirad by dastardly means and since then it has been the haunt of all kinds of ogres and evil spirits, which set upon any who enter the valley. Be careful, therefore, not to set foot in it, because even if you escaped alive, all my sheep would certainly be taken and, if that happened, you would have to answer for it with your life.'

Jaroslav promised to carry out the Duke's command, and, well pleased, returned home to his sheep. From then on, he lived the peaceful, happy life of a shepherd. Often he would take his zither and play on it, till all the sheep were skipping and gambolling like lambs, so he knew that what his father had said about its powers was true; but being a kind-hearted fellow he would not try out the ivory rod, even on an animal, but was content to assume that it too would do as the pilgrim had said.

That winter was a long and difficult one, and, when spring came at last and freed Nature from the bonds laid upon it, there was little grass left for the royal sheep to graze; but, oh how green were the hillsides of the forbidden valley. There was rich grazing there for many sheep, and the young shepherd regretted that he was forbidden to take his sheep there. They would have liked it so much. Then, one night, Jaroslav dreamed that a tall, noble lady with a shining helmet on her head, dressed in a long, flowing silken gown, over which she wore a breastplate of gleaming steel, came and stood at the side of his bed and said:

'You stupid youth, why do you not follow the prompting of your inner voice and go into the valley, where much good fortune awaits you? Why let the fears of an old man keep you from great honour and fame?'

Then the figure vanished and Jaroslav woke up. All the rest of that night he lay awake thinking of his strange dream, and in the morning, when he let the sheep out, he drove them in a direction they had never taken before: towards the forbidden valley.

As Jaroslav entered the valley he had his zither slung round his neck and in his satchel lay his ivory rod. His sheep began at once to graze the lush rich pasture and they had gone far among the blossoming trees, when round the shoulder of a hill came a man so tall, that the shepherd reached no higher than his waist. His skin was black and his features twisted and ugly. He wore a black cloak that fluttered round his

shoulders and in his right hand he carried a huge
ebony cudgel. In a fearful voice the giant called:
'You impudent dwarf, how dare you enter my
territory? Didn't I forbid all of your hated race to
approach my palace? Death shall be your punish-
ment.'

Saying that, the giant lifted his cudgel aloft and
advanced towards Jaroslav with the obvious intention
of knocking his brains out. But Jaroslav just took his
zither and began playing a gay dance tune. At the
sound of the first bar, the giant dropped his cudgel
and at once began to skip about and dance. On and
on Jaroslav played, till the giant fell exhausted to the
ground; then Jaroslav produced his ivory rod and
touched him with it, and that was the end of the giant.

Being a thoughtful young man – and rather inquisi-
tive – Jaroslav went through the giant's pockets and
in one of them found a golden key. Ha, he thought,
somewhere in this valley there must be a lock which
this key fits, and I should like to see what is behind it.
So, gathering his flock together, he strode off in search
of such a lock.

After about a quarter of an hour he came in sight
of a marble castle and going up to its great door, he
found that his key fitted its lock. He opened the door
and walked through into a courtyard. Facing him was
a stable door and, hearing a whinny, he went inside
and saw a wonderful black horse that pawed the floor,
as though tired of doing nothing. Jaroslav liked the
look of the horse so much, that he led it out into the
yard, swung himself up and rode round and round
the great courtyard for a while, then he led the black
horse back into its stable.

Next, Jaroslav went inside the palace itself and wandered through its magnificent apartments till he came to a great hall hung with costly rugs. In the middle stood a round table on which lay a great sword, a goblet and a crystal bottle full of dark wine. On the table itself the following was engraved in letters of gold:

'If you drink this goblet full of wine, you will be able to wield this wondrous sword, the blows of which no shield can parry.'

Beside the table, laid out on black velvet cushions was a complete suit of finely-wrought black armour, with shield and lance. Jaroslav felt a great desire to try it on, but something held him back. Then he tried to pick up the great sword, but he could not get the point more than an inch or two off the table. He wanted to drink up the wine and see if that would have the promised effect, but an inner voice told him that the time would come when he would have need of that promised strength, and he refrained. So he went out again into the great courtyard, and, seeing his sheep crowded round a low door, he went across and opened it. The moment he did so, a hundred black lambs came pouring out and mingled with his. So off Jaroslav went back the way he had come with a flock considerably larger than that with which he had left home that morning.

As luck would have it, the Duke arrived to inspect his flocks just as Jaroslav reached home. Seeing the black sheep, as he could not fail to do, the Duke sent for Jaroslav and asked whose they were. Jaroslav, looking very innocent, said:

'Who could they belong to, Your Grace, but you?'

Then the Duke's brow clouded and he said:

'I see that you have been disobeying my orders and have risked my flocks and your own life in order to satisfy your curiosity.'

'Forgive me, Your Grace, but I was only looking into the valley from a mound and saw the black lambs gambolling without anyone to look after them. When they saw my sheep, they came and joined them and so I drove them home together.'

The Duke, who was not reluctant to have acquired a hundred sheep for nothing, wagged his finger at Jaroslav and said:

'I will forgive you this time, but my order not to enter the valley stands and I would advise you not to disobey it.'

Having proved the wonderful powers of his zither and ivory rod, Jaroslav felt sure that he had no need to worry about losing the ducal sheep and so had no need to obey the Duke's order. He now wished to explore the valley more than ever, so, one sunny morning a few days later, he again made for the valley. This time he drove his sheep past the marble palace, he had visited before, and soon came to a flat stretch of ground ringed by gentle hills. In the middle of it he saw another giant, even bigger than the last, coming towards him. This giant was of normal colour and dressed in ordinary homespun, and in his right hand he swung an enormous sickle of bright steel. When still a good hundred paces away, the giant asked Jaroslav what he was doing there. Jaroslav, feeling rather pleased with himself answered back:

'Now, now, big man, don't fuss. I've come here because I want to and I am going to graze my sheep on this lush grass today. So just you leave me alone, and I'll leave you alone.'

This cheeky answer made the giant speechless with fury. He opened his mouth and raised his sickle, but at that moment the gay notes of the tune Jaroslav was playing on his zither reached his ear, and he dropped his sickle with a clatter and began to dance and hop, so that the ground shook. And so it went on: Jaroslav played and the giant danced, on and on until finally Jaroslav's right arm grew so tired he could play no more. At that the giant, who was tired too, but not yet exhausted, picked up his sickle and aimed a sweeping blow at Jaroslav; but Jaroslav darted forward and dived between the giant's legs, touching him with his ivory rod as he did so. The giant dropped to the ground with an appalling thud – dead!

Again, Jaroslav went through the giant's clothes and this time, too, he found a key, cut from a single jewel. Taking the key, he walked on and soon came to another castle. This one was built of crystal. The key opened the great door for him, and, inside, he found a stable with a fine white horse and a shed full of white sheep. Within the castle itself he discovered another complete suit of splendid armour and a table, its top engraved with the words: 'Drink of this wine and you will be able to stand up to the devil himself.' On the table stood a bottle of white wine.

Jaroslav inspected and admired it all, then went out again, closing the door behind him. For a while, he stood wondering whether he should add the white sheep to his flock or not; then, telling himself that the Duke was unlikely to come and make another inspection for some time, he decided to take the sheep, which, being white, the Duke would probably never notice, when he did come. So, adding the giant's flock to his own, Jaroslav drove his sheep home.

Unfortunately, on his way he encountered the Duke, who was returning from a hunt, and the Duke could not help seeing that his flock had grown considerably.

'How dare you disobey my orders a second time,' roared the Duke, outwardly angry, but secretly quite pleased that he had acquired another hundred sheep or so for nothing. Jaroslav flung himself to the ground and begged for forgiveness, which the Duke with feigned reluctance, granted, threatening him with the direst penalties if he sinned again.

For many days Jaroslav kept away from the giant's valley in obedience to the Duke's command; but he felt drawn to it and so did his sheep, which much preferred the giants' grass to that of their rightful owner. So, one morning, when the sheep of their own accord set off towards the valley, Jaroslav let them go and strode gaily after them.

On they went past the two palaces to where the valley narrowed. There a roaring mountain torrent foamed between tall cliffs, bringing the path to an abrupt end. Leaving his sheep, Jaroslav clambered on upstream along the cliffs, determined to go on till he found further adventures. He had not gone far before he came in sight of another castle, so deep red in colour it looked as though made of solid ruby. The castle seemed to be empty. Somewhat disappointed, Jaroslav sat down on a hummock and began strumming on his zither. He had not played long before an enormous figure appeared above part of the battlements, more gigantic even than the owners of the other two castles in the valley. The giant's face grew red with rage as he caught sight of Jaroslav. Raising aloft a great sword, which glowed as though it was red hot, the giant strode through the gate and came rapidly towards the hummock, where Jaroslav sat. As soon as Jaroslav saw this, he began to play a dance tune. The giant was in the act of stepping across the torrent, when the music reached him; instantly the sword fell from his hand and dropped hissing and sizzling into the depths of a pool, and then this giant too began to hop and skip about in a lumbering dance. Soon, however, Jaroslav stopped playing and the giant, without bothering about his sword, made straight for the intruder, hand out-stretched to grab him and dash his brains out against the rock. Such was the giant's intention, but Jaroslav had his ivory rod and the moment the great fist approached, he just touched it with the knob and the giant's knees sagged and he toppled over dead, with a crash that sent some loose rocks tumbling down the cliff face.

In his haste, the giant had forgotten to close the gate of his palace, so, seeing this, Jaroslav did not bother to search his pockets for a key, but swam the stream and climbed the far cliff to where the castle stood. As he entered it, a huge red stallion came whinnying up to him. It nuzzled him and unprotestingly let him lead it back into its stable.

In this third castle, Jaroslav found the same round table and on it a bottle of red wine, and another suit of armour made of some metal that was unknown to him and so bright it almost hurt his eyes to look at it. The table bore the following inscription in letters of red:

'Once the glow of the wine gets into your blood, Victory will never fail you. Even the devil will admit you his master.'

Jaroslav inspected and admired it all, but obedient to the prompting of his inner voice, he took nothing with him, when he left the castle – but a flock of red sheep, whose wool was so fine and thick that he just could not resist the temptation of adding them to his flock. After all, he was a shepherd.

Naturally, the red sheep were such an unusual sight that everybody talked about them, and before long a messenger came spurring out to order Jaroslav to go at once to the Duke.

This time the Duke was really angry. It was not that he did not want more sheep, but he did want the people in his service to obey him, and this was the third time that Jaroslav had deliberately disregarded his orders. That had to be punished. So, it was a grim-faced Duke who received Jaroslav and told him that he was dismissed from his post as ducal shepherd and henceforth was to be assistant to the old gardener who looked after the ducal pleasure gardens. Jaroslav was too frightened to protest, much though he disliked the idea of digging and weeding instead of roaming about with his sheep; so he had to go back home, pack up his things and return to the city, where, the next morning he reported to the old gardener for duty.

Jaroslav liked gardening and worked so well that everyone praised him. Often, however, during the midday rest, he would find himself longing for the country and wishing he were exploring the forbidden valley. At such times he would softly play a tune on his zither, sad little melodies of longing. Now it happened, one warm June evening, as he stood by the greenhouses singing softly and accompanying himself on his zither with a sweet, but melancholy air, the Duke's young daughter came for a stroll in the gardens and heard him. Coming closer, she saw the handsome young gardener for the first time and thought him the nicest and best-looking person she had ever seen. After that, the Duke's young daughter often asked her father to send for the assistant gardener in the evening and get him to sing for them, which Jaroslav gladly did, accompanying himself on his magic zither, so that in no time at all the Duke's daughter had quite lost her heart to him.

One morning, when he arrived for work, Jaroslav found the old gardener with tears coursing down his face. Asking what had happened, he was told the sad story of how long years before the Duke and his Duchess had been childless. They had prayed and prayed, gone on pilgrimages to the most efficacious shrines and consulted all the great physicians of Bohemia and far beyond, but nothing had helped. Then, one day, there had appeared in the fair city of Prague a man of swarthy complexion, who wore sombre but costly clothes and said he was a learned physician from the far land of Persia. He had heard, he said, of the Duke's great sorrow and come to help him. There was a secret conference at which the Duke, rather stupidly, had signed a document in his own blood agreeing that his first child should become the property of the physician if and when they reached the age of seventeen. The Duchess had then given birth to three children, of whom only the eldest, a girl, was alive. This was the girl Jaroslav knew and she was almost seventeen. The previous day the Duke had received a message from the physician, whom he had hoped never to see again, claiming his daughter and requiring that she be brought to a certain spot outside the city and handed over to him on her seventeenth birthday.

Jaroslav was horrified. He could not bear the thought of the lovely girl, whom he now loved so deeply, being given to an old man who was obviously a wizard, if not something much worse. Then he remembered the forbidden valley of the giants and the magnificent suits of armour and bottles of wine with their strange promises and he determined to try and save the Princess. So, on the morning of the day when the Princess, attired and garlanded like a bride, was to be led to the meeting-place, Jaroslav begged the morning off to go, as he said, and watch, promising to tell the old gardener all about it the moment he got back.

Leaving the city by a side gate, Jaroslav hurried to the forbidden valley and entered the first castle. He went at once to the stable, saddled the horse and led it out. Then, entering the castle, he went to the great hall, put on the suit of armour and, draining the bottle of wine, found that he could lift the huge sword with the utmost ease.

Calm and dignified, the Duke's daughter sat on her horse as she rode with her father, her maids and attendants to the decreed rendezvous. The church bells rang, but it was a dirge they tolled, not a joyful wedding peal, and the wretched girl's heart was heavy. As the company reached the appointed spot, a knight in splendid armour appeared. Across his shoulders was a cloak most magnificently embroidered with gold and in his hand he held aloft the agreement they had made so that all could see the Duke's own signature at the bottom. The Duke was just about to hand the reins of the Princess's horse to the grim figure of the knight, when a shout rang out and, turning, they all saw a knight in black armour, mounted on a splendid black horse, come spurring out from a side valley. He brandished a huge sword and called upon the knight to hand back the girl.

The evil knight turned swiftly and, eyes flashing, said:

'Who are you, mortal, to dare tell me to give up my rights?'

'I am here to defend an innocent girl against the evil that you are. And to do so I am prepared to fight you and all Hell, if need be,' said Jaroslav with considerably more confidence than he really felt.

The bad knight was only too ready to accept this invitation and called to Jaroslav to dismount, so that they could fight it out on equal terms.

Then began such a fight as none of those present had ever seen. Metal rang, sparks flew as blade struck blade, and feet stamped as the two adversaries circled round each other, slashing, thrusting, chopping. In the end, the evil knight cried:

'Enough for today. Let us continue the contest tomorrow.'

Jaroslav, who was almost done, was very glad to agree and while the Duke, grateful for at least a postponement, led his daughter back into the city, Jaroslav rode back to the castle, doffed his armour and putting on his own clothes, ran back to the city, where he gave the old gardener and his wife such a graphic account of the proceedings that their old eyes goggled.

The next morning, Jaroslav again begged leave of absence and, hurrying to the second castle, put on the suit of white armour, drank the wine and, mounting the great white charger, reached the rendezvous just as the Princess arrived. The next moment they saw a huge dragon approaching, spewing flames from its four heads and calling upon Jaroslav in the voice of the evil knight to stand and fight.

Fortunately, the white armour seemed impervious to flame but every time Jaroslav chopped off one head of the dragon another grew in its place. Soon the ground was littered with smoking dragons' heads, but the dragon was able to accomplish nothing and eventually suggested postponing the fight until the following day, when they would decide it. Again Jaroslav agreed and mounting his horse, rode back to the valley, without giving the Duke or his daughter an opportunity to thank him or question him. So, the Duke took his daughter back to the city for at least one more night at home.

Again Jaroslav returned and thrilled the gardener and his wife with a blood-curdling account of the fight. In the morning, the old gardener was only too glad to let him off again and Jaroslav hurried to the third castle and donned the third suit of armour and, mounting the great red horse, he rode to the meeting-place. As he reached it, the ground opened, flames roared up and the evil knight appeared. Undismayed, Jaroslav dismounted and prepared to fight.

It was a tremendous battle. For a long time neither seemed to have the advantage, but at last, the evil

. . . a huge dragon approaching, spewing flames from its four
heads . . .

knight's sword fell from his hand. Jaroslav ordered him to produce the contract with the Duke, took it and burned it before his eyes. Then there was a roar and the evil knight vanished. Jaroslav turned and walking to the Duke's daughter knelt before her.

During the fight, the evil knight's sword had pierced his left arm-piece and bitten deep into the flesh. The wound was bleeding profusely and, just as Jaroslav was about to speak, he swooned and rolled over at the girl's feet. There was a great commotion. People rushed up to help. They removed the arm-piece and the Princess herself tied up the wound with her own silken handkerchief. Then she and her father rode back to send the ducal physician to attend to her rescuer.

In the meantime, however, Jaroslav came to his senses, and, getting to his feet, mounted his horse and rode off before anyone could stop him. Reaching the castle, he changed back into his own clothes and went back to the garden.

When the Princess heard that her rescuer had disappeared, she was sorry indeed, because she would so much have liked to thank him. The next day, in glorious sunshine, she went for a walk in the gardens and, turning a corner, saw the young gardener stretched out asleep on the grass. She looked and looked, unable to believe her eyes, for there on the gardener's left arm was her own silk handkerchief. Wondering, she woke Jaroslav and he, feeling that fate intended all this to happen, told her the whole story.

Though, of course, she did not say so, the Duke's daughter was overjoyed to find that the young man she secretly loved so dearly was also her rescuer, and dragged him off at once to her father. The Duke, half convinced, told Jaroslav that the handkerchief was not quite proof enough of so incredible a tale, so Jaroslav, promising to come back soon, ran to the first castle in the valley of the giants and, putting on the suit of armour, mounted the great horse and rode to the Duke's palace in the city. The Duke and his daughter at once recognized their champion on the first day, and, when the knight removed his helmet and they saw the grinning face of the assistant gardener, all doubt was swept aside. The Duke overwhelmed him with thanks and told him to name his own reward. But seeing the looks the two young people gave each other, he realised without being told and gave orders for the wedding to be celebrated that very day.

In due course, the old Duke died and Jaroslav and his fair wife ruled in his place. And very well he did it. He was kind and understanding and not really very strict – except about sheep-stealing.

FOURTEEN

The Whirlwind's Captive

A KING AND A QUEEN had a daughter, their only child. She was a pretty baby, a lovely little girl and by the time she was seventeen, when this story begins, she was really beautiful. Her hair was like spun gold. Like many other fathers and mothers, before and since, this King and Queen were terrified lest anything happen to their lovely daughter and they went to absurd lengths to protect her and keep her from harm: she was not allowed out of the royal apartments, nor to meet anyone but the ladies-in-waiting and governesses appointed to look after her. Yet despite the fact that she never went anywhere or did exciting things, or even met new people she was always happy and gay and good-natured. She had lovely clothes and beautiful jewellery, and seemed perfectly content.

Then, when the Princess was eighteen, whether by chance or by the intervention of Fate, it happened that she heard the cuckoo for the first time. And surely it must have been Fate, for what other pretty girl whose sitting-room and bedroom window opened on to a garden the size of a park, could have reached the age of eighteen without hearing a cuckoo a thou-

sand times? Anyway this new sound struck some chord
within her and she sat by the open window so lost in
thought or daydreams that she did not even hear her
mother come into the room. The Queen had come to
tell her daughter something rather important: she
and the King had decided it was time for the Princess
to choose a husband and they had now sent invitations
to all the young Princes of the neighbouring kingdoms
to come and visit them, so that she could see and talk
to them and decide which she liked best. The Princess
was delighted at the idea and kissed her mother
happily.

When the Queen had gone back to her own apartments leaving her daughter to her thoughts and
dreams, the Princess went back to her seat by the
wide window and suddenly felt an irresistible desire
to go into the garden and walk on the green lawn on
which she had never yet set foot. She called her ladies-
in-waiting and was so insistent in her request to be
allowed to go out, that they could not refuse her. So,
the doors were opened and the Princess entered the
gardens for the first time in her life.

The sun was shining, birds were singing and
insects buzzing and the princess was delighted. The
smells enchanted her and the feel of the soft grass
beneath her feet. Then a butterfly flitted past and
she ran off after it and was soon out of sight of
her middle-aged, short-winded ladies-in-waiting. She
lost sight of the butterfly, but ran on darting from
flower-bed to flower-bed, smelling and picking flowers,
dancing and pirouetting as she ran along. Her face
was radiant with happiness and she had never looked
so lovely. Then, out of the blue, a whirlwind, spinning

. . . a whirlwind . . . seized hold of the Princess and carried her off

and roaring, swept down upon the garden, seized hold of the Princess and carried her off.

The poor ladies-in-waiting wrung their hands in despair, turned and ran back to the palace, where, weeping and sobbing, they told the King what had happened. The Princess's parents, stunned by this dreadful news, did not know what to do; in fact they were still racking their brains when the young Princes they had invited began to arrive. Seeing the King and Queen in the depths of despair, they naturally asked what had happened, and the King told them the terrible news and how no one had any idea where the whirlwind had taken their daughter, nor how to find her. Desperately, the King promised that the Prince who could find her should have her for his wife, with half his kingdom and also inherit the other half on the death of the King and Queen.

Hearing this, the Princes leaped on to their horses and rode off in search of the missing Princess, asking everyone they met if they had seen the whirlwind or the Princess. Two of the Princes, who were brothers, searched together, riding side by side, but nowhere could anyone give them any news of either the whirlwind or its victim. Month after month the two Princes rode and at the end of many months they came to a great mountain, so high its top was hidden in cloud. Something told them that this was where the Princess was, and, dismounting, they began to climb. When they came within sight of the top, they saw a palace made all of silver and built on a pedestal shaped like a cock's foot, and in one of the windows they saw a head of hair, so golden that it could only have been the Princess's. Their hearts leaped with joy at the discovery, but at that moment a fierce north wind began to blow. The cold became so intense that their breath froze and the trees cracked and split. Before long, the two Princes were overcome and dropped lifeless to the ground.

Meanwhile, the two Princes' parents waited anxiously for their return. Then one day a beggar came to their palace and was taken into the big hall and given shelter. He said that he had a message for the King and Queen, both bad news and good. First, that their two sons were lying frozen on the mountain and only a miracle could save them, but, for their comfort, he could also say they were going to have another son, who would be truly great and do noble deeds no one else had ever done.

Some time later, the Queen gave birth to a baby, a boy but no ordinary boy, for his eyes were like a falcon's, his eyebrows like a martin's, his right hand was of pure gold and his whole bearing majestic and commanding. The rest was equally wonderful when only three days old he leaped from his cradle and ran to meet his parents. Seeing their troubled faces, he asked why they were unhappy and they told him about his brothers. Hearing this, the baby said:

'Don't worry. By next spring I shall be a strong young man. I'll search the world and find my brothers and bring them back to you.'

The King and Queen were surprised to say the least of it. But the boy did grow at an astounding pace. A month later, he was an excellent swordsman, and by the time another month had passed he had learned to ride, and shortly after that he had grown a moustache of pure gold.

One day, the young lad put on his helmet and breastplate of steel, took his sword and dagger and went to the King and Queen:

'My dear parents,' he said, 'As you see, I am now a grown man, a child no longer; so I shall go and search for my brothers. Give me, please, your blessing.'

The young Prince looked so strong and handsome that, though in their heart of hearts, the King and Queen were reluctant to let him go, they gave him their blessing and wished him luck in his quest. So, the young Prince with the golden hand mounted his horse and rode off. He rode for many days crossing deep rivers and climbing tall mountains, then he came to a dark and gloomy forest and, there, in a great clearing he saw a small house built on a foundation shaped like a cock's foot. Surrounding it was a field of poppies, all in flower. As he approached it, the young Prince felt suddenly terribly sleepy and he could scarcely keep his eyes open; but, spurring his horse, he swept through the field of poppies, breaking their heads as he went, and pulling up before the cottage, he cried:

'Cottage, cottage, that I see. Turn about and face your door to me!'

At that there was a creaking and groaning and the cottage swung round on its cock's foot pedestal and stopped with the door facing the Prince, who at once walked through it. Inside he found an old woman with white hair, her face covered with wrinkles and splodges, which made her truly hideous. She sat at a table, her head in her hands, eyes fixed on the ceiling, seemingly deep in thought. Beside her, on a bench, sat two girls. They were both young and pretty, with rose-pink complexions and merry eyes. They were really worth looking at.

'Welcome, Prince with the hand of gold. What brings you to me?' said the old woman, whose name was Yaga.

The Prince told her of his quest. Then she said:

'Your brothers perished on the mountain that reaches the clouds, while looking for the golden-haired Princess, whom the Whirlwind carried off.'

'And how shall I find the Whirlwind?' the prince asked.

'Oh, poor young man! The Whirlwind will crush you like a fly. Even I am afraid of him. I haven't left this cottage for a hundred years for fear he will carry me off to his mountain.'

'But he won't carry me off, and he won't crush me, because I have a golden fist that can smash everything.'

'Well, if you're not afraid to try, I'll help you. Only promise me that you will bring me some Water of Youth, which makes those sprinkled with it young again.'

'I will, indeed.'

'Well, this is what you must do. Take this ball of wool which will guide you. Just throw it in front of you and wherever it goes, you follow. It will take you to the high mountain which, if the Whirlwind is away, is guarded by its relations the North Wind and South Wind. If, on the mountain, you feel suddenly cold, put on this warming cap. A bit higher up, you may run into suffocating heat, then take a drink from this refreshing flask. With these three things to help you, you'll get to the top, where the Whirlwind has im-

prisoned the Princess with the golden hair. As to how
you will deal with the Whirlwind, that is your affair.
Only, remember to bring me some Water of Youth.'

The Prince took the cap, the flask and the ball of
wool, said good-bye to Yaga and her two pretty
daughters, jumped into the saddle and throwing the
ball ahead of him, rode off in the direction in which it
went rolling.

Across two kingdoms the ball led him and into a
third, and in the midst of this one he came to an
extensive valley of great beauty from the centre of
which rose a high mountain, whose summit was so
high above the clouds it seemed to reach almost to
the moon. Realising that this was the place for which
he was looking, the young Prince dismounted and
turning his horse loose to graze, he set off up the steep
mountainside after his guiding ball.

The slope was steep and stony and the going was
hard. He climbed and climbed, and, looking up
realised that he was still only half-way. Then, all at
once he felt a cold wind on his face. The wind became
more and more violent and the cold so intense and
piercing that the wood in the trees cracked and the
young Prince's breath froze on his moustache. Feeling
that he was about to succumb, the young Prince
pulled the old woman's cap from his pocket and
clapping it on his head, cried:

'Warming cap, warming cap, give me warmth and
keep the cold from harming me.'

At that the North Wind blew with redoubled fury,
yet the cap warmed so well and made the young
Prince so hot that he broke into a sweat and had to
unbutton his coat and mop his face.

All at once, his guiding ball stopped on a hump of snow. The Prince scuffled the snow aside and uncovered two frozen bodies, which he felt sure were those of his two brothers. He knelt beside them and said a prayer; then the ball moved on and he followed it. After a while the silver palace came into view and he recognised the foundations built in the shape of a cock's foot. Looking up at the windows he saw the sun glinting on a golden head of hair, which could only belong to the Princess for whom he was searching. At that moment, he felt a blast of hot air on his face and the sun seemed to beat down with double the strength. Fiercer and fiercer, hotter and hotter became the wind; the leaves began to shrivel, the grass to wither and cracks appeared in the earth. The heat was so sudden and so fierce, that the Prince was almost overcome by it, before he remembered the flask that old Yaga had given him. Now, taking this from his pocket, he cried:

'Flask, come refresh me and keep me from harm!'

He drank off a deep draught and felt vigour flood back into him. Then he climbed on, no longer aware of the heat, in fact he felt so cold that he had to button up his jacket.

The ball was still rolling on ahead of him, and thus together they crossed a stretch of the eternal snows and reached the top of the mountain. There he found the palace, a most wonderful palace, for it was made of silver, with steel grills over the windows and a golden roof, the whole building resting on a great pedestal shaped like a cock's foot. The door and porch faced a chasm, so deep that no mortal being could approach them; yet there, at one of the windows, was the princess, golden hair shining and glinting as it stirred, eyes bright and sparkling. Seeing her, the Prince darted forward, crying:

'Palace, palace turn on your foot. Back to the chasm. Door to me!'

Then, slowly and with much creaking and squeaking, the palace began to turn on its cock's foot pedestal till the door was facing the Prince, who opened it and strode inside.

No sooner was he inside than the door shut and the palace swung back into its former position, trapping him inside.

The Prince found himself in a big room which was dazzlingly light, for the walls and ceiling and floor were of mirror, and seeing twelve princesses all equally beautiful, all having the same expressions, making the same gestures, in the same attitudes, he gaped. Then he realised that only one was real and the other eleven were just her reflections.

Seeing the Prince, the Princess uttered a cry of joy and ran towards him:

'Oh,' she said, 'you are just like an angel come to save me. I'm sure you bring me good news. Who are you? Where do you come from? And why have you come? You haven't been sent by my father or mother, have you?'

'No. I have come on my own to rescue you and return you to your parents,' he said and went on and told her all that had happened and how it was that he had come. The Princess listened and then said, rather sadly:

'I am grateful indeed and glad you have come. May God bless you for your sacrifice. But whether you can do anything, I very much doubt. The Whirlwind is invincible and fortunately not here at the moment, so, if you value your life, I would advise you to go back where you came, while you still may. When the Whirlwind returns, he will kill you with a single look.'

'If I do not succeed in rescuing you, what use is life to me?' said the Prince, gallantly. 'But I am confident, especially if you could get me some of the strengthening water the Whirlwind drinks.'

The Princess hurried to the well which served the Whirlwind and drew a bucket which she took at once to the Prince. He emptied it at one draught and asked for another, which he emptied at the same speed, to the considerable surprise of the Princess. Then he said:

'Might I sit down for a moment to get my breath?'

She indicated an iron chair in which he seated himself, but it shivered into a thousand pieces beneath him. Then she brought him the chair that the Whirlwind himself used and though this was made of steel it bent complainingly beneath his weight.

'You see,' said the Prince. 'I have become heavier than your invincible Whirlwind, so be confident that with God's help I shall defeat him and rescue you. Now, while we wait for him to come back, tell me what it is like here.'

'Well,' said the Princess, 'it is horrible and I am most unhappy. You see he pesters and pesters me to become his wife and I loathe him. I have told him that I can only marry a person who can guess six riddles that I have made up and he has been trying to guess them for two years now in vain. Now, he has told me that if he isn't right the next time he tries, he will marry me by force – so, you see, you have come just in time and I am most grateful and glad.'

At that moment they heard a terrible whistling sound.

'There you are,' said the Princess. 'Look out! He's coming!'

The palace began to revolve swiftly on its queerly shaped pedestal, and a dreadful clamour arose as thousands of ravens and birds of ill-omen began croaking and cawing and all the doors in the Palace opened noisily of their own accord. Then into the door where the two sat, swept the Whirlwind mounted on a winged horse that breathed fire through its nostrils. The horse reared up at the sight of a stranger and beat its wings.

The Whirlwind was of gigantic stature and his head was that of a dragon.

'What are you doing here, stranger?' he called in a voice like the roar of a lion.

'I am your enemy and I have come for your blood,' the Prince replied coolly.

'Well, I admire your cheek, I must say,' said the Whirlwind. 'But, even so, if you don't leave at once, I shall put you on my left hand and crush you with my right till there's not a bone of you left.'

'Just you try it, you bully!'

The Whirlwind went purple in the face with fury and flung himself at the Prince, mouth open and spewing fire, ready to swallow him up. Nimbly, the prince leaped aside and, thrusting his golden hand into the Whirlwind's open mouth, seizing his boasting tongue and with a great tug sent the Whirlwind hurtling against the wall with such force that he smashed his skull and his brains poured out.

The Prince took the half-swooning Princess in his arms, then he filled three bottles with water from each of the three wells he found in the courtyard, one with the water that gave back life, one with water that gave back youth and one with water that gave extra strength and vigour. He took the winged horse, which was standing there as firm as rock, by the bridle and cried:

'Palace, palace, turn about; open the door and let me out!'

Creaking and groaning the palace turned till the back was facing the chasm and the door opened on to the mountainside. The Prince led the winged horse outside and mounted it with the Princess still in his arms. Then he cried:

'Horse of fire do my will. I am your master now. Carry me in the direction in which I am pointing.'

Then he pointed to where the frozen bodies of the two princes were lying. The great horse, reared up, beat its wings and flew off, to alight gently at the place where the bodies lay. The Prince with the golden hand sprinkled his brothers' bodies with the water that gives life and at once the stiffness left them, colour poured back into the cheeks, then they opened their eyes and, sitting up, looked around them.

'Well, we've had a good sleep,' they exclaimed. 'But how's this? The Princess with the golden hair with an escort we don't know. What's happened?'

The Prince with the golden hand quickly told them who he was and what had happened. Then he and the Princess mounted the horse, his two brothers got

up behind him and the Prince pointed his hand of
gold at the place where Yaga's cottage stood. The
horse took off, beating its great wings, and flying high
above the forest, was soon at the cottage.

When they had landed in the field of poppies the
Prince said,

'Cottage, cottage turn about. Let your door be
facing me.'

Then the cottage began to turn with much rusty
creaking and squeaking, and the door appeared facing
the little group. Then the door opened and old Yaga
came out to greet them. The Prince gave her the flask
of the Water of Youth and sprinkling herself with it,
all that had been old and ugly about her vanished
and she stood there young and charming. She was
so delighted that she kissed the Prince's hands and
said:

'Ask me for whatever you wish. I can refuse you
nothing.'

At that moment her two young pretty daughters,
as fresh as roses, looked out through the windows and
the two older Princes, seeing them, cried:

'Give us your daughters for our wives.'

The now young Yaga laughed and said:

'You shall have them,' and she signed to the girls
to come to their future husbands. Then, seeing that
the great horse looked capable of carrying even two
more the girls were told to pack a small bundle
each and then, with everyone mounted, the great
winged horse took off again in the direction in which
its master's golden hand was pointing.

Again the great horse flew so high, that it almost
reached the clouds. Then, a couple of hours later, it

began to glide down to earth and landed gently in
the very garden from which the poor Princess had
been carried off by the Whirlwind. Out ran the courtiers, out came the King and Queen and when they
saw their beloved daughter back again, they too
broke into a run, and soon she was in their arms.
Then they all went into the palace, where the whole
story had to be told.

When they had heard all there was to tell, the King
said:

'Well, we made a promise and we shall keep it.
You, Prince, shall have our daughter for your wife,
half my kingdom and inherit the rest when I die. As
your brothers want to marry too, let us have a triple
wedding.'

Then the Princess with the golden hair kissed her
father and said:

'There is one thing yet. As my fiance knows, to
save myself from the Whirlwind I vowed that I would
only marry a man who could guess the six riddles
that I had made up. Having made the vow, I cannot
very well break it now, can I?'

The King looked disappointed, but he said nothing.
The Prince, however, said:

'Come on, then! I'm ready to try.'

'Well, here's the first,' said the princess: 'Two of
my eyes form a sharp point, the other two a ring and
the middle is a screw.'

The poor Prince looked quite blank. Then his face
flushed with embarrassment, he looked at the ground
and shuffled his feet, thinking desperately. But he
could not think of a thing. Then he happened to catch
sight of the Princess's hand hanging at her side. The

first and second finger were making a movement like
a pair of scissors snipping at a thread.

'Scissors,' said the Prince, looking up.

'Well guessed,' said the Princess, giving him a lovely
smile. 'Now here's the second: On one foot I make
the round of the table; but if I am knocked over, all
is lost.'

Again the poor Prince's face remained blank. He
could not think of what hopped round the table on
one foot. Hopefully he looked at the Princess's hands,
but they were still. Then, he shot an appealing gaze
across the Princess's shoulder at his brothers and saw
one of them raise his hand to his mouth as though
drinking. For a moment he did not understand, then
he did:

'A beaker of wine,' he cried in relief.

'Well done,' said the Princess. 'Now, listen, this is
the third: Although I have no tongue, I give a faithful
reply; no one sees me but everyone can hear me.'

The Prince's face was radiant as he exclaimed:

'An echo.'

'That's right. Now, the fourth: Fire does not light
me, broom does not sweep me, no painter can paint
me, no place hide me.'

Again an expression of bewilderment came over the
Prince's face. His golden hand came up and scratched
his head. He looked down at the floor and up at the
ceiling; then, as he looked down again, the Princess
took a step forward into a shaft of sunlight, which fell
straight on her face. The Princess looked straight up
it towards the window through which the sun was
streaming, and the Prince's face beamed in a triumphant grin:

'Sunlight!' he said.

'Quite right,' said the Princess. 'Now for number five. I existed before Adam was created. I am always changing the two colours of my garment. Thousands of years have passed and I have not changed in any way, neither in shape nor colour,' and saying that the Princess turned her head and looked at the great clock on the wall.

Silence. No one spoke. Everyone stood looking at the Prince. He looked at the clock, thought and thought, looked at the Princess, who looked at the clock again, then a hesitant smile appeared on the Prince's face and he said:

'Time?'

'Yes, time alternating between day and night. You are clever! Now, those were difficult. The sixth and last is much easier. Here it is: Round by day, serpentine at night; who guesses what it is shall be my husband.'

Imperceptibly the Princess's hand dropped and her thumb began to play with her belt.

'A belt,' said the Prince, and the Princess ran across and kissed him, then taking his arm she led him to where the King, her father, and the Queen sat, and the two knelt before them to receive their blessing.

A mounted messenger was sent to tell the parents of the three princes of their safe return and to invite them to the weddings. When they arrived, the three couples were married, and there was much feasting and merry-making and, as far as I know, they all lived very happily, as most people do.

FIFTEEN

The Mysterious Shepherd

ONCE THERE WAS a Prince, who had three handsome young sons of whom he was very proud. He wanted them to be real Princes and do all the princely things, fighting for their country, looking after its people and helping in the government. This the two older ones were perfectly happy to do, but the youngest insisted that he wanted to be a forester and nothing else. The Prince, his father, was furious and ordered him to put that idea out of his head. The young Prince, however, was obstinate and rather impertinent and they had a noisy quarrel, at the end of which the Prince's father said:

'All right, go and be what you want to be, but not in my territory. Get out!'

And the young Prince gave him a furious look, which he hoped was cold and haughty, and said:

'All right, I will.' Then he put on a suit of ordinary countryman's clothes and set off out into the world.

The young Prince's name was Hynek.

Hynek soon found that it was one thing to be a Prince and like the idea of the simple life, and quite another to be a young man without money in search of a job in a strange country. He was cold and very hungry, and felt that everything and everyone was against him. But Hynek really was a nice fellow. He was fond of Nature and animals and all the simple things, and genuinely disliked life at court. Finally, he became so tired that he just lay down under a tree and fell fast asleep. As he slept, a black man came along and seeing Hynek, bent down and shook him awake. Hynek had never seen a black man before and he was rather frightened at first, but he soon realised that the man was a good man, whatever the colour of his skin, and the black man liked the look of Hynek and took him back to his house in the woods. There Hynek stayed for seven years, during which time the black man taught him seven languages, as well as to play the zither and all sorts of other accomplishments.

Now, in that part of the world there was a fierce dragon that could only be appeased and kept from ravaging the towns and villages by periodical gifts of a human being and a sheep. When the time came for a new gift to be made, the people used to draw lots. Such a dreadful time was at hand and the lot this time had fallen upon the King's only daughter. The black man and Hynek agreed that something must be done to free the people from the persecution of the dragon and to save the Princess. Then the black man thought out a way and told Hynek to go to a near-by farm and ask to be taken on as a shepherd, and then in the morning, to drive the sheep into the forest, where the black man had his house.

Rather puzzled, Hynek did as he was told, and, to his joy, found that the farmer was glad to take him on. In the morning, then, he drove the sheep into the forest, where he found the black man waiting for him. The black man gave him a ring and a wand.

'If you turn this ring on your finger, you will be taken to a castle, where a giant lives. You must kill the giant. The wand will help you tackle him. Having killed him, you must take his cloak, his sword and his horse, and turn the ring again. You will, then, find yourself on the road near the town, along which the Princess is to be brought. The rest is up to you.'

Hynek took the wand and the ring and found that everything worked as the black man had said: he was close to a big castle and as he approached, the giant appeared in the gateway.

'Ha! You miserable earthworm,' he exclaimed, 'what are you doing here.'

'Me? Oh, I've just come to have a try for that big head of yours,' said Hynek.

This reply infuriated the giant, and he flung the great club he was holding at Hynek, who dodged it in time and it hurtled on and buried itself in the ground. Hynek darted in and struck the giant with his wand, and the giant toppled over and fell to the ground. Then Hynek snatched up his sword and cut off the giant's great head. He searched the giant's pockets and finding an iron key, went inside, unlocked the giant's chest and dressed himself as befitted a noble knight; then he led the giant's horse from the stable, mounted and turned the ring once again.

The next moment Hynek found himself on the high road down which they were bringing the Princess on her way to the dragon. When the procession drew abreast of him, Hynek asked:

'Ha! You miserable earthworm,' he exclaimed, 'what are you doing here?'

'What on earth's happening and why is everyone so sad and gloomy?'

They explained about the dragon and how the Princess was the one on whom the lot had fallen and they were taking her to be handed over.

'Not if I can help it,' said Hynek. 'I'll gladly risk my life for one so beautiful. Show me where the dragon lives.'

They pointed to a great cliff-face and Hynek rode over to it and called out in a loud voice:

'Come out, dragon. Your meal is here, waiting for you.'

But the dragon called back:

'I don't want it today. Come back tomorrow at eleven.'

So Hynek rode back and told the Princess that the dragon was not coming out that day and they all returned to the city. The Princess took Hynek to her father, and the King begged him to stay, but he made all sorts of excuses, then he turned the ring on his finger and found himself back in the giant's castle. He changed back into his shepherd's clothes, stabled the horse and put everything tidily away, then he turned the ring again and found himself back in the forest, where the black man had been tending the sheep.

Hynek told the black man all that had happened and what he had done, and the black man was full of praises:

'You have done well. Always act like that.'

Then Hynek drove the sheep back to the farm for the night. That evening at the farm, Hynek played his zither and everyone came crowding round, drawn by the magic of it, but, of course, Hynek did not tell them anything about the giant or the Princess.

The next morning, Hynek again drove the sheep to the forest, where he found the black man waiting as before.

'If you just do as I say,' said the black man, 'you will be happy and successful. Today, you must deal with another giant and then see whether the dragon will come out or not. Take the ring and the wand as before, and, remember what I have told you. I'll look after the sheep, while you're away.'

So Hynek took the wand and the ring, and turning the ring on his finger, found himself outside another castle, looking up at a great giant, who was standing in the gateway.

Grimly, the giant asked him what he wanted.

'Nothing much,' said Hynek. 'Just that big head of yours.'

The giant was holding a hammer and he now hurled this at him, but fortunately he missed and Hynek leaped forward and struck him on the leg with his wand, whereupon the giant collapsed and fell to the ground. Hynek whipped his sword out of its scabbard and cut off his head.

This giant had a silver key in his pocket, which Hynek used to unlock his chest and array himself as befitted a noble knight, then he led out the giant's horse, girded on his sword, mounted and turned the ring.

Again Hynek found himself on the high road, with the Princess's procession approaching. Going up to the sad-faced attendants, Hynek, speaking a different language, asked why they were all so sad and what was happening. As before, they told him the sad story of the dragon's persecution and the drawing of lots, and how it was the Princess's turn to be sacrificed.

Hynek looked at the Princess and said:

'Not if I can help it. I will gladly give my life for one so lovely. Show me where the dragon lives.'

The people pointed out the cliff-face, at the bottom of which was the entrance to the dragon's lair, and watched the strange and handsome knight ride across to it. Then Hynek called out:

'Come out, dragon. Here is your meal waiting,' and the wind carried the words to the Princess and the halted procession.

Then the dragon replied:

'I don't want it today. Come back tomorrow at eleven.'

So again the Princess was reprieved and they all rode back into the city, where the King again did his utmost to persuade her champion to stay; but the strange knight made excuses and, wheeling his horse, rode off again. Then he turned his ring and, back in the castle, stabled his horse, put the clothes all back and returned to the forest with another turn of his ring. There, the black man again praised him and said:

'Drive the sheep home now, but come back tomorrow and a little earlier, for an even heavier task awaits you then.'

Hynek was so afraid of oversleeping that he scarcely slept at all that night. As soon as day began to break, he urged his flock out with much baaing and meh-ing, and drove them to the forest, where the black man was already waiting for him.

'This is the last day,' said the black man, 'but it will

take you all your time to deal with both the giant and the dragon. Anyway, here is the wand and the ring, you know how to use them. The giant will have a golden key in his pocket. You must take the black horse in his stable and when you have killed the dragon, bring me the sword you did it with. Now, off you go and good luck.'

So, Hynek turned the ring and was transported to the ground outside yet another castle. In the gateway stood a giant, even taller and broader than either of the others. The moment he saw Hynek, he came running at him, but he was so huge, it was easy for Hynek to dodge out of the way and rush in and deal him a smart blow on the leg with his wand. The giant crumpled up and dropped to the ground, where Hynek killed him with his own sword. Then he went through the giant's pockets till he found the golden key, opened the giant's chest and got out a green cloak and a suit of magnificent clothes that could not possibly have fitted the giant, because they might have been made for Hynek; then he went to the stable, led out a magnificent black horse he found there, mounted it and turned his ring.

Again Hynek found himself on the highway a little way from the Princess's city, from the gateway of which a cavalcade was just emerging. Hynek waited till it approached, then he rode up and, speaking yet another language, asked the sad-faced people what was the matter and why they all looked so doleful. They then told him about the dragon and the Princess and how the lot had fallen on her and again Hynek very gallantly said that he would gladly give his life to save someone as beautiful as the sad Princess – who blushed when he said that and looked at her – and then he asked where the dragon lived. A forest of eager hands pointed to the great cliff, and riding over to it, Hynek called out:

'Come out, dragon. Your meal's here, waiting.'

Then the earth began to quake. Stones came rolling down the face of the cliff and a trickle of earth fell. There was a great rumble, then a roar like a clap of thunder and the dragon rushed out. It was no ordinary dragon, for it had seven heads, each ringed with leaping flames, and each so horrid and fierce it would have been more than enough for even the most self-respecting dragons. It rushed straight at Hynek who, using the giant's great sword, began chopping off the heads as fast as he could. But the ghastly thing was that as one went rolling and bouncing across the turf, scorching the grass, another grew in its place.

So the fight went on, the great black horse wheeling, backing and leaping forward as the dragon advanced or retreated, while Hynek hewed and slashed till he felt that his arms would drop off. In the end he could scarcely raise the sword and he thought he would have to admit defeat. Then, all at once, his big black horse gave a whinny so loud that the sound of it rebounded from the cliff-face and went echoing down the valley; then rearing up, it began fighting the dragon with its fore feet, slashing and stamping to such effect that the dragon had to back away, seeming to find it quite as formidable an opponent as the knight on its back. While the horse fought, its iron-shod hooves striking sparks from the dragon's scales, Hynek rested. Then, feeling that strength and vigour had returned to him, he raised his great sword aloft again and with one great sideways slashing blow struck all seven heads off at a go. That finally killed the dragon, which slowly sank to the ground, while the dancing flames round its seven heads slowly died down and went out.

With the intense heat and the tremendous effort of that final great blow, Hynek fainted and toppled to the ground from his great horse. The members of the Princess's cavalcade, who were watching from a safe distance, came spurring up and, picking him up, carried him away, in case he should be harmed by the dragon's poison. They brought him to where the Princess, who had dismounted, was sitting and laid him down beside her with his head in her lap. They fanned his face and before long he opened his eyes and was rather embarrassed – and pleased – to find himself lying with his head in the Princess's lap. The Princess gave him a ring from her finger and the gold chain she wore round her neck, and said that he must come back with her to the city and meet her father. But the Princess's rescuer insisted that he could not stay, he had duties to attend to, he said, but he promised to come back within three days. So of course, they had to let him go.

So, Hynek rode away for a short distance, then used his ring to return to the giant's castle, where he stabled the great black horse and put everything back in its place, except the sword which he kept in his hand as he turned the ring on his finger for the last time and had himself transferred to the forest, where the black man waited for him, tending his sheep. He gave the black man the sword and described all that had happened, and the black man told him:

'You have succeeded most excellently and now all will be well with both of us.'

Then Hynek drove his sheep home, feeling wonderfully pleased and happy. He felt so gay, that he got out his zither and played, and everyone crowded round to listen and applaud. Then, pretending that he did not know, he asked what had happened to the Princess and was told that a strange knight had killed the dragon and rescued her and that the King wanted the knight to marry her.

'Oh,' said Hynek, 'I ought to have tackled the dragon with my shepherd's staff. I would have knocked its heads off.'

But they all laughed and told him not to boast, but to stick to shepherding.

Meanwhile, in the royal palace, they made great preparations for the return of the strange knight who had rescued the Princess. The Princess and all her ladies were frantically cutting and pinning and stitching to make new dresses, and, down in the kitchens, the cooks were baking and roasting in preparation for the wedding banquet that was to be held as soon as the knight arrived.

But the days passed and there was no sign of the knight, nor any word from him, and the Princess grew sad and her father looked puzzled. Then, on the sixth day, when they were talking at the farm about the failure of the knight to turn up and how sad the Princess was, the shepherd asked if he might have the day off and go and play his zither to the Princess, because maybe that would cheer her up. The farmer gave him permission, on condition that they shared any money the shepherd was given, so the next morning, the shepherd took his zither and walked to the palace. There he played his zither, and his playing was so sweet and lovely that everyone had to listen, including the Princess. He played and played, then he said that he must be going. Some of the lords asked him what reward he would like, and he said:

'Just to drink a beaker of wine with the Princess.'

The court musicians were furious with him for asking for so little and muttered to themselves that they would not let him play there again, but the lords applauded him and the royal cup-bearer was sent for a beaker and a jug of wine. Then he filled the beaker and handed it to the zither-player, who drained it and into it dropped the ring the Princess had given him and which he had been holding ready. When he handed back the beaker and the cup-bearer was going to fill it for the Princess, he saw the ring and showed it to the Princess, who, of course, recognized it at once and ordered the shepherd to be brought to her.

Then the Princess asked the handsome zither-player, how he had got the ring, and he told her that he had been the knight on each of those three days. The Princess was overjoyed and took Hynek straight to her father, who welcomed him as his son-in-law and sent for the royal tailors to make him some presentable clothes. They sent word to the farmer not to expect his shepherd back.

The Princess and her father could see that Hynek was not of lowly birth, as a shepherd lad would be, but the Princess had fallen in love with him, and her father was so grateful to him for rescuing his daughter, that neither bothered to ask who he was and Hynek's head was in such a whirl with all that had had happened to him recently, that he never thought to tell them things about himself.

They had a lovely wedding and were very happy together. One day, the Princess said that she would like to meet her husband's parents, and Hynek decided that it really was high time he took his bride home and introduced her; but, because of his quarrel with his father he did not want to do it in a simple and straightforward way. So he had a letter sent to his father saying that a certain Princess would be visiting him on a certain day.

Then they set out, but the Princess travelled alone with her suite and Hynek went on ahead, dressed in his old shepherd's clothes. Back at home, he mingled with the crowd waiting to see the Princess arrive, and when she went inside he followed with some of the others. When the King saw a man in rather ragged shepherd's clothes standing there, and recognised his son, he was furious that he should have turned up like that and gave orders that he should be taken and locked up. Hynek had no difficulty in escaping and entered the great hall just as they were coming in for a banquet. He went and sat down beside his wife. His father, red in the face with anger, apologised profusely, but the Princess assured him that she did not mind, in fact, she said, she was glad to have him beside her however he was dressed. The King, of course, just thought she was being polite and swore to himself that he would punish his son for this scandalous behaviour.

After the banquet, Hynek slipped upstairs and into the Princess's room and there he changed into his proper clothes, which his wife had brought with her, and together they went to see the King and told him the whole story.

What the King would have said, or what he would have done, there is no knowing, but just as Hynek finished speaking there was a flourish of trumpets and in strode the black man. Going up to Hynek, he drew his sword and handed it hilt first, to Hynek and asked him to cut his head off. Hynek naturally protested, saying that he owed everything to the black man and could not repay his kindness by killing him. But the black man insisted that if he did not do as he asked, they would both be most unhappy; so, rather hesitantly and reluctantly, Hynek took the sword and with one great hissing stroke, severed his benefactor's head from its black neck. The Princess began to scream, but stifled her cries because, suddenly, where the black man had been, there now stood a youth of eighteen, who announced that he was an English Prince who had had a spell put on him, while travelling in Bohemia, and only now been rescued.

You can imagine everyone's surprise and rejoicing, especially when the young Prince's companions, who had also been under a spell lying asleep in a cave, suddenly came looking for him. Well, to cut a long story short, Hynek and his young wife decided to go with the Prince back to England, but whether they got there or whether they ever came back, I do not know.

SIXTEEN

The Twin Brothers

ONE DAY, when a woman went down to the river to fill her pail, she saw a silvery fish swimming about in the shallows. 'That would make a nice meal for me and my husband,' thought the woman and was just about to try to catch it, when the fish, to her great surprise, spoke in a human voice and told the woman that it was really a Princess who had been turned into a fish by a wicked sorcerer.

'If you will rescue me from this enchantment, you will have twin sons,' said the fish.

Now the woman had always wanted children, but she had none, so she told the fish that she would do anything if her dearest wish, to have children of her own, could be granted.

The fish replied, 'You must catch me and bury me in your field and plant a rose bush over my body. When the roses bloom in the early summer-time, you will have twin sons. When the boys are five years old, you must dig where I was buried and there you will find two fine steel swords. When the boys are ten years old, your mare will have twin foals and your bitch two pups, so your sons will each have a horse and a dog, when they are growing up. The swords will enable them to vanquish any enemy; so, when they are both sixteen, they must go forth to seek their fortunes.

'But long before that the sorcerer's wicked spell will be broken and I shall have turned into a princess again as soon as my body has rotted away.'

All turned out as the fish had promised, and when the two brothers were nearly grown up they decided to set out to seek adventure, so saying good-bye to each other and to their parents, they set off in different directions. Before parting they agreed to look at their swords each day, for if ever one saw that his had started to rust, he would know that the other was in danger and needed help.

One brother rode off into the forest and after a while he noticed the trees were withered and the ground all parched and stony, while a peculiar, acrid smell hung in the air. Suddenly he heard a slither and a rattle and a loud hiss, and out from scorched-looking trees waddled a hideous, bloated dragon with nine venomous heads. It reared up and would have crushed the youth and his horse if he had not drawn his magic sword and severed two of its heads with a blow. Frightful, smoking blood welled from the two necks, but the other heads darted and snapped and hissed with redoubled fury. Then began a terrible fight beneath the silent trees. The young man hacked and hewed at the dragon's heads, with his fearless agile horse helping him with all its might, and at last the horrible swollen body lay lifeless on the ground with its nine severed heads around it. The young man left the heads as they lay, but he cut out the tongues and put them in a bag. Then he cleaned his sword, mounted his horse and rode quickly away from the sinister battleground.

Some woodcutters had heard the sounds of fighting and had felt the earth shake and they journeyed to the place where the dragon lay dead. Now for many years this dragon had been a curse to the kingdom, for each time it went to the town it would choose one victim to eat. This time it was known that the Princess was to be its next victim and all the buildings were draped in black and the people mourning for their Princess. The King had promised his daughter in marriage to anyone who could kill the dragon and this the woodcutters knew. All of them were too humble to falsely claim the Princess as their bride, except for one boastful fellow who boldly picked up the dragon's heads and set off for the town, announcing that he was sick of being a woodcutter and would be the Princess's husband instead.

When she saw who was claiming her hand, the Princess was horrified. He was a coarse ugly man and she felt that she could never marry him, but her father could not go back on his word, so plans for the wedding were arranged, but the Princess and her royal parents insisted on the most elaborate arrangements and kept changing their minds and altering things, just in order to put off the evil day as long as possible.

During this time, the brother who had killed the dragon rode into the town on his beautiful horse and stayed at the inn, which was very crowded. All the guests were talking about the Princess's wedding and wondering when it would be, and the young man listened to all their talk.

When he had heard the story he asked: 'Is everyone

sure that it was the woodcutter who killed the dragon?'
and they all answered, 'Oh yes, because he brought
the dragon's nine heads!'

The young man said nothing, but he went to the
palace and asked to see the man who had slain the
dragon. When the woodcutter was brought to him, he
asked him to show him the dragon's heads. He looked
at them and asked.

'Did you really kill the dragon?'

'Indeed, I did,' replied the man.

'And what did you kill it with?'

'With my axe.'

'You are a liar,' replied the youth firmly. 'No axe
could have severed those heads!'

The woodcutter began to bluster and protest, but
the young man asked him why there were no tongues
in the heads.

'The dragon didn't happen to have any tongues,'
lied the woodcutter and at that the young man pulled
the nine dragon tongues from his bag and showed them
to the company.

The Princess was overjoyed not to have to marry
the woodcutter, who was driven out of the town in
disgrace. And she was much impressed by the young
man's handsome looks and proud bearing, and so they
were married and lived very happily together.

But the Princess's husband was still the adventurous
young man he had always been and he could see from
his window, in the far distance, a black castle standing
among jagged mountains. To all his inquiries, he was
only told that the castle was enchanted, and no one
who had gone there had ever returned. This made him
all the more eager to go, and have a look at the castle

and he turned a deaf ear to his young wife's pleas that he should stay with her and not risk his life in such a perilous adventure.

One morning he ordered his horse to be saddled and with his dog following, he rode out from the palace towards the forbidding mountains. The journey was so difficult that anyone less brave would have turned back. The ground was broken by deep cracks from which foul-smelling mist curled up and his sure-footed horse was hard put to it to jump across them safely. At last they reached the great iron gates of the black castle, which opened into a dark, shadowy courtyard. All around were the figures of men and animals who had been turned to stone. The young man and his dog entered the castle and there sat a wrinkled old woman crouched over a fire. She drew back shuddering as they entered and in a snivelling voice whined, 'Dear Lord, tie up your dog. He might bite me. You don't want to hurt a poor, lonely old woman. Tie him!'

'Do not fear,' replied the young man. 'He will do you no harm.' He bent down to pat his dog and at that moment the old hag sprang, as quick as a snake, and struck him with her wand. And he and his horse and his dog were all turned to stone.

The Princess waited for her husband, but he did not return and she and the people of her kingdom, who loved him too, mourned his death.

Now the other brother noticed that his sword had started to rust, which was a sure sign that his twin was in trouble. He rode forth to find him and came to the town where the people were mourning for their lord. When they saw him they thought it was his brother returning, especially as he had a horse and a dog just like their lord's and they joyfully took him to the Princess who was equally certain that this was her husband who had come back. She asked why he had not returned sooner and he pretended that he had been captured by robbers in the forest and held prisoner until he escaped.

The Princess would have been very happy, and her husband's twin was careful not to say that he was only the brother, but he never would kiss or embrace her, and the Princess was very upset and puzzled by his strange attitude to her. One day he also noticed the black castle from his window and questioned the Princess about it. 'I have already told you,' she replied. 'No one ever comes back from there and it's a good thing the robbers did capture you before you ever got there, or you would probably be there still!' Then, at last, the young man knew where his brother had gone.

Without telling anyone, he took his horse and his dog and rode off on the same perilous journey to the black castle. As soon as he entered the iron gates he saw his brother with his dog turned to stone and all the other knights and their horses like statues. And he, too, came to the old hag sitting by the fire. 'Stand!' he commanded her 'and bring my brother back to life, or I will hack you into little pieces with my sword!'

The old woman knew the sword was magic and she was afraid. She grovelled and whined. 'Don't be angry, dear sir! Take this little box of ointment and rub some of it beneath your brother's nose and he will soon be restored to life again.'

'No,' he shouted, 'you shall do it!' and seizing her wand he struck her across her shrinking shoulders. At that instant she turned into an ugly, twisted, little statue of stone.

He had not realised the wand would do this and rather fearfully he took the box of ointment and rubbed some of it beneath his brother's nose and to his joy he was restored to life. Then they went round doing the same for all the knights and their animals who had been kept there under such cruel enchantment and then they rode back to the palace where the Princess was waiting anxiously.

When she saw them both, alike as two peas, she did not know which was her husband.

'Alas!' she faltered, 'What am I to do, for which of you is my true lord?'

They smiled and asked her to choose the right one, but she blushed and shook her head and was unable to see any difference between them. At last they laughed and put her out of her difficulty, her real husband stepped forward and took her in his arms. Then at last she knew that this was her true love and they held a great feast to celebrate the victory of the two brothers over the wicked enchantress in the black castle. Afterwards the bachelor brother set off for further adventures, and the Princess and her husband lived happily ever after.

SEVENTEEN

The Twelve Months

WHERE THE STREAM that tumbled down from the hills was just getting big enough to be called a river, there stood a pretty cottage in a sweet little garden. In fact, the cottage was really big enough to be called a house, and in it lived a widow and two girls. The younger girl, Mary, was the widow's own daughter and the elder, Helen, her stepdaughter, her late husband's child by a previous marriage. The widow was a bad, nasty person. She did not love her stepdaughter and was very jealous of her because she was so much prettier than her own daughter, Mary. Helen, who was nice and generous, could not understand why her stepmother was so often angry with her and gave her all the hardest and nastiest household jobs to do; in fact she did most of the work: turning out the rooms, cooking, washing, making and mending, spinning and weaving, looking after the cow and other animals, while Mary just sat in front of her mirror, preening and prinking with very little justification, because she was really rather plain.

Helen's patience and good humour only made the other two angry and spiteful, so that the poor girl was far from happy. However, she grew more and more beautiful as she grew up and her stepsister plainer and plainer. One day, the widow said to herself: 'Somehow or other I must get rid of Helen, because as long as she's in the house no man will look at my dear Mary.' Between them, the widow and Mary made a plan: they would make life so unpleasant for poor Helen that she would run away. So they heaped more and more work on the poor girl, said nasty, horrid things to her and did their best to make her unhappy but Helen accepted it all and never complained, even when they refused to let her have supper and sent her to bed hungry.

One day, in the middle of winter, when the snow lay deep on the ground, a wicked thought came into Mary's mind. Turning to her mother, as the three were sitting at the fire, she said:

'I do wish I had some violets. Couldn't Helen go up the mountain and get me some.'

'But, sister, violets don't flower in winter, in the snow,' said Helen.

'Now don't you contradict,' said the widow. 'You are to go up the mountain as your sister says and don't you dare come back without a nice big bunch of violets for us. If you do, I'll kill you.'

Poor Helen was quite taken aback by the ferocity in her stepmother's voice and dared say nothing more, so, taking her cloak she got herself ready to go.

Mary and her mother almost pushed her out of the door and slammed it behind her. Then they looked at each other and grinned gleefully. Mary even danced a couple of steps across the kitchen floor.

As she walked away from the house, Helen's eyes filled with tears. She could not understand why they were being so unkind and it was so silly to think she could find violets in the depths of winter. But what was she to do and where was she to go? It was too cold to stand still, so she set off walking across the snow on which there was not a footprint, not so much as the track of an animal. All was still and cold, and for a long time Helen wandered about getting colder and colder and more and more hungry. Then it began to snow again and the poor girl felt really desperate, but she just wandered on and finally emerged from the trees to find herself on the mountainside. Looking up, through the falling snow she saw a light, and she set off towards it. Up and up she climbed. The light never seemed to get any nearer, while the slope just became steeper and steeper. Soon her knees were aching and she was puffing and panting, but she struggled on, because where there was a fire surely there would be people, especially when the fire was in such a strange place; if there were people, someone would surely help her.

Finally, Helen saw that she was nearly at the top of the mountain and there on a little platform under the peak itself blazed a huge bonfire, in the middle of a circle of big stones that at that moment were serving as seats for twelve men. Three were old and white-haired, three were middle-aged, three seemed in their prime, young and very handsome, and the others were quite youthful, one, in fact, only a child. Helen was delighted and relieved to see them, and far too tired and worried to be at all surprised at their sitting there.

As the girl approached, none of the twelve moved or looked up. Nobody spoke, they just sat staring into the

Looking up through the falling snow she saw a light . . .

fire, their faces flushed with the heat of the great blaze, which Helen too could feel, if only just enough to make her wish she could get closer. In the end, when still no notice had been taken of her, she plucked up courage and turning to the oldest of the twelve, who was seated on a stone a bit higher than those of the others, said:

'Please may I come a little closer. Because it is so cold and I am beginning to shiver.'

Now, the twelve men were really the Twelve Months, and the name of the one to whom Helen had spoken was January. Raising his head to look at Helen, January said:

'What are you doing here? Why have you climbed up all this way?'

'I am looking for violets,' Helen replied.

'But it's not the season for violets. Not with snow lying everywhere. Don't you know that?'

'Yes, I do,' Helen said, 'but my half-sister Mary and my stepmother have told me to bring them a big bunch of violets and that if I come back without them, they will kill me. Please, tell me where I could find some.'

Then old January rose up to his full height and, walking round the fire to where the youngest month sat, gave him the baton that he held and said:

'Brother March, take the high seat.'

Then March got up and went and sat on the high stone seat and waved his baton over the fire, and at once the flames flared up till they were licking at the clouds and the ring of light from the fire moved far down the mountainside. Then Helen saw the snow melt, the bushes and plants begin to bud and burst into leaf, the grass become green and here and there among it, she saw primroses. Then she looked again and there, under some bushes, were violets. She looked up at March, wondering, and when she looked down again she saw that the ground was blue.

'Hurry and pick your violets, Helen,' said March.

And Helen did. Delighted she stooped down and walked about picking and picking, till her hands could hold no more. Then she went and thanked the Twelve Months, especially young March, and set off down the mountain, happy to be going home however unkind and nasty her stepmother and sister were.

Mary and her mother had been hoping that they would never see Helen again, either because she would not have the courage to come back without the violets they had ordered her to get or because she would have been overcome by hunger and cold. Great then was their surprise, when the door opened and in the doorway they saw Helen's smiling face and an enormous bunch of violets, their glorious smell flooding through the whole house.

'Where on earth did you get those?' Mary asked, too surprised to be angry at the failure of her plan.

'Away up on the mountain, just under the peak,' Helen replied. 'The ground was quite blue with them.'

The others looked incredulous, but there were the violets to show that Helen was speaking the truth. Mary snatched the violets from her, held them out for her mother to smell and carried them off to her room without saying thank you or letting Helen keep even one for herself.

A day or two later, spoilt Mary had a sudden

yearning for strawberries, fragrant wood strawberries with lots of sugar and cream, and calling for Helen, who came hurrying from the woodshed where she had been working, she said:

'Helen, just run up on to the mountain and get me a bowl of big ripe strawberries. And make sure they are sweet.'

'But, goodness gracious, you know you don't get strawberries in wintertime,' Helen said.

'Don't you answer back,' snarled Mary. 'If you got violets, you can get strawberries. Now, off you go.'

'And don't you dare come back without them,' said her stepmother, 'or we'll kill you. Won't we, Mary?' Then she took poor Helen by the shoulders and pushed her outside.

Helen could only hope that she would find the twelve months on the mountain and that they would be willing to help her again. There had been another fall of snow and the white surface was quite unmarked, but Helen knew her way. She had only to walk on uphill, up and up till she reached the top.

Before long Helen emerged from the line of tall trees on to the mountainside, where the snow was grey beneath a leaden sky and the bushes all weighed down by fat caps of snow. You could not imagine a more unlikely place in which to find strawberries. But Helen trudged on up the mountain. In some places the crust of the snow was hard enough to bear her, but in others her feet went right through it and before long she was wet to the waist and quite breathless with floundering in the deep drifts. But she struggled on, growing more and more anxious every time she looked up without any sign of the heartening light that would tell her that the Twelve Months were there again, seated round their fire.

Helen had almost reached the top before she saw the comforting glow of a fire a short distance away and, as she drew nearer, made out the ring of stone seats and the Twelve Months sitting on them. Again January occupied the high seat of honour. This time, Helen did not wait, but walked up to the old man and said:

'Please may I warm myself at your fire, for I am shivering?'

And old January looked at her and said:

'What have you come here for?'

'I am looking for strawberries, big ripe wood strawberries,' Helen said.

'But this is the middle of winter. Strawberries don't grow in the snow,' January said. 'Surely you know that?'

'Yes, I do,' Helen replied, 'but my stepmother and stepsister will kill me if I come home without any. So, please, please, can't you help me?'

January stood up and walking to the month who sat facing him, gave him his baton and said:

'Brother June, you take the high seat.'

So June went and seated himself on the tall stone and, then, leaning forward, he swung his baton above the fire and at once the flames went soaring and roaring up into the sky and the heat was so intense that Helen covered her face with her hands. When, after a while, she dared remove her hands from her face, she saw that the snows had vanished, the earth was green, the bushes covered with leaves; birds were singing and there were flowers everywhere. It was summer and beneath the first line of trees, some great beeches, the ground was studded with white stars that, as she watched, turned into strawberries that ripened in an instant. There was a whole field of them.

'Hurry, hurry,' exclaimed June, 'go and pick them.'

Helen was only too glad to do so and soon her apron was so full of them she could carry no more. Then, looking round, she thanked the Months for having helped her again and hurried off home.

Mary and her mother were looking out of the window watching the sunset, and saw Helen coming. They ran and opened the door for her and, as she stepped inside, the whole house was filled with the fragrance of wild wood strawberries.

'Where on earth did you find them?' Mary and her mother asked together.

'Up on the mountain,' Helen replied. 'There are lots by the big beech trees there.'

Mary took charge of the strawberries. She gave some to her mother, but never thought of letting Helen have one. But Helen did not mind. As long as she was not turned out into the cold, the others might guzzle as much as they liked.

A day or so later, Mary decided she would like a nice red apple and again mother and daughter drove the unhappy Helen out of the cottage, despite her protests, promising to kill her if she dared to come back without some nice red apples.

This time Helen felt really desperate, because she dared not even hope that she might find the twelve months a third time. And if she did, why should they help her again? So, sniffing and crying and feeling dreadfully sorry for herself, she wandered off through the woods; but, luckily for her, her feet took their own direction – uphill. Soon Helen emerged from the belt of beech trees on to the face of the mountain itself and there, away up by the summit, she could see a point of light that sometimes shrank till it almost disappeared and sometimes swelled till she could almost see the leaping flames. So, stumbling through the deep snow, Helen climbed the mountain a third time and finally came to where the Twelve months sat, still and silent, on their stone seats, gazing into the fire. None of them looked up as she approached. None moved or spoke, but they all sat, motionless, gazing into the glowing heart of the fire. Then, Helen went close to January and asked his permission to warm herself at the fire, and again January asked what she was looking for and why she had come, and, when she told him that she was looking for apples and would be killed if she went home without them, which she dared not do, January got up off his seat and handing his baton to another of the Months, whose hair was already grey, said:

'Will you, September, please take the high seat.'

So September got up and walked across to the high seat and swung the baton above the fire, sending the flames leaping into the heavens and colouring the ground red. Again the snow disappeared, buds appeared, burst into leaf and the leaves began to fall and a cold breeze sent them swirling and dancing across the ground, all yellow and brown and red. The only flowers to be seen were meadow-saffron and such autumn ones. Helen looked and looked, but nowhere could she see any apples, till, all at once, she saw one tree that had a few scarlet apples right at the top.

'Hurry, hurry,' exclaimed September, and Helen ran to the tree and began trying to shake it. At last she dislodged one apple and then after a few more shakes another fell to the ground and rolled to her feet.

'That's enough,' said September. 'Hurry back home.'

So Helen picked up the two apples, thanked September and the other Months for their help and ran through the forest back home.

Mary and her mother were surprised enough to see the apples, but the next moment Mary's angry voice was asking why Helen had brought so few. No doubt she had eaten a lot on her way down?

'No, indeed, I haven't even tasted one,' Helen said. 'The first time I shook the tree one fell, and then I managed to shake another down, but they wouldn't let me go on shaking, but told me to go home.'

'You've eaten them, you mean thing,' said Mary and raising her hand, slapped poor Helen's face.

Helen burst into tears and ran into the kitchen, so miserable she almost wished she had never gone back home, but had died instead.

When Mary bit into one of the apples, she discovered that it was quite the loveliest she had ever tasted and her mother thought so too. And how they wanted more!

'You know, Mother,' Mary said. 'I'm going to get those apples myself. I shan't be put off by anyone telling me not to shake the tree as that poor fool, Helen, seems to have been. Give me my fur coat and a basket and I'll go and clear the lot.'

The widow did not think this a good idea, but her daughter would not listen to her, and insisted on putting on a warm bonnet, a fur coat and a thick pair of gloves, then, picking up a big basket, she walked off. Her mother stood in the doorway anxiously watching till she was out of sight.

The surface of the snow was unmarked. There was not a track to be seen, not a sign to show Mary which way Helen had gone, so she wandered about for a long time before she caught sight of the fire on the mountain above and set off in that direction. Stumbling and floundering she made her way up to the top and was somewhat taken aback by the sight of the ring of seats and the Twelve motionless figures seated on them, but, being pert and pushing by nature, she went up, thrust her way in between two of them and stood by the fire warming herself, without even bothering to say how-do-you-do or ask if she might.

Then January in a deep, hard voice, said:

'Who are you and what brings you here?'

'What's that to do with you, you old grey-beard,' Mary retorted. 'You mind your own business and I'll mind mine.' Then, feeling that she was warm enough, Helen turned and walked off to look for the apple-tree.

Frowning, January waved his baton above his head and in an instant the sky had filled with leaden clouds, snow began to fall in great flakes and an icy wind was loosed and went sweeping, roaring down the mountain. So cold that no fur coat could keep its wearer warm with such a wind blowing. The wind howled and Mary cursed her silly sister for not telling her exactly where the tree was, but determined to find it.

Hours later, Mary's mother was still at the window staring out in the direction in which her daughter had gone. More and more worried, the widow finally decided to go and look for her daughter, so she fetched a shawl and a cloak and, wrapping up as warmly as she could, opened the door and stepped out into the cold. The swirling, falling snow had covered up all tracks and there was nothing to show which way Mary had gone. So the widow roamed about, calling and calling, then pausing to hear if there was an answering cry. But the only sound was the wind in the trees and a soft thud as a lump of snow slid off a branch and fell to the ground.

Meanwhile, at home, Helen had milked the cow and shut up the hens. She had peeled the potatoes and got supper ready, when it suddenly struck her that the house was strangely quiet and still. There was no one there. She was alone.

Now, no one could have blamed Helen if she had been glad that her tormentors had gone; but she was such a nice, good-natured girl that she really felt sorry for them and looked outside and called and called into the silent night, in case she could help. The wind had died away and the snow stopped falling. Her voice must have carried a long way, but there was no answer to her calls and at bed-time, as neither had returned, Helen put out the lights and went to sleep.

All the next day Helen waited, expecting that one or other might return, but they never did, for both had frozen to death on the mountain, and serve them right.

So, the house and little farm became Helen's and she looked after everything as best she could, until one day she fell in love with a handsome farmer's son and he married her and came to help her, and, with four hands to do the work, life became the gay and happy thing it ought to be.

And when Helen had children of her own, they could never understand why their mother did not like wood strawberries violets or apples.

EIGHTEEN

The Three Hairs of Dedewshevede

LONG, LONG AGO there was a King of Bohemia who was such a keen hunter and had such a wonderful horse, that he was always out-distancing the others and finding himself alone in the forest. Usually he knew where he was and could find his way home alone, but on the day when the story begins, he had lost his way and was overtaken by darkness in the depths of the forest. Coming to a charcoal burner's hut, he asked the man if he would guide him to the highway, for which service he would reward him handsomely. The man, being poor, would gladly have done so, but, he explained, his wife was about to have a baby and he dared not leave her alone. Why, he suggested, did the King not spend the night where he was? He could have a soft and fragrant bed of hay in the loft, on which he could not fail to sleep well, and in the morning the charcoal burner would guide him where he wished.

The King agreed and having supped, retired to bed. No sooner had he done so than he heard the cry of a new-born baby.

At midnight the King woke up and was surprised to see light shining through the gaps in the planks of the floor and the sound of voices in the room below. Lying down, he was able to look into the room below and saw the charcoal burner asleep, his wife stretched out beside him, and three old women, dressed in white, standing round the baby's cradle. Then he heard one of the three say:

'I grant this child the gift of tackling the greatest dangers.'

The second said:

'And I the ability to survive them and a long life.'

And the third said:

'And my gift is that he shall marry the Princess born at the same hour as he to the King who sleeps in the loft above.'

At that, the light went out and there was silence.

The King was horrified and spent the rest of the night wondering how he was going to prevent the prediction of the third of the Fates from coming true, for he realised that that was what the old women were. As day broke, the baby began to cry and the charcoal burner woke up. Then, to his horror, he discovered that his wife was dead. Going to the King he asked in despair what was to become of the baby.

'Give it to me,' said the King, pretending to be very kind and generous, 'and I'll see that it is properly treated. And I'll give you enough money to help you along, too.'

The charcoal burner was delighted. He guided the King to the highway, and the King rode off promising to send for the baby that same day. When he reached home, he found the Queen and all the courtiers waiting for him, eager to tell him the glad news that he now had a daughter. But, to their surprise, the King just frowned. Then, calling one of his most trusted servants, he gave him some money, told him to give it to the charcoal burner in exchange for his baby and to take the baby and drown it.

'And, if you don't do it properly,' said the King, 'you shall be drowned instead.'

The servant took the baby in a basket and rode away from the charcoal burner's cottage. He did not have the heart to drown the baby, but just threw the basket into the river at a place where the current was strong and watched it being swept away rapidly, till it was out of sight and bound, he supposed, for the great waters of the Black Sea.

Fortunately for the baby, the current sent the basket swirling into the bank just where a fisherman had his cottage. The man fished the basket out of the river, saw the baby in it and took it to his wife. They were a childless couple and overjoyed at this unexpected gift, and the fisherman's wife loved the baby at once and looked after it, as if it had been her own.

Years passed and the baby grew into a handsome young man. One hot summer's day the King, who had again out-distanced the hunt, came to the fisherman's cottage and asked for a drink of water. The young man brought it to him, where he sat astride his horse. The King looked at him attentively, then, turning to the fisherman, said:

'You have a fine-looking lad there. Is he your son?'

'Yes and no,' said the fisherman, and explained how he had fished a basket with a baby in it out of the river some twenty years before.

Hearing this, the King became as white as a sheet,

The man fished the basket out of the river . . .

for he realised that this must be the charcoal burner's son. When he had recovered himself, he dismounted and said:

'I need someone to take a message to the castle. Could you send your son for me?'

'Only too gladly,' said the fisherman.

So the King sat down and wrote a messàge to the Queen. This is what he wrote:

'The young man who will bring you this message is the most dangerous of all my enemies and you must have him beheaded at once. Have no pity. Grant no respite. He must be executed, before I return.'

He folded the letter, sealed it and gave it to the young man, whose name was Plavacek.

Plavacek set off at once, but darkness fell before he was out of the forest. There he met an old woman, of whom he asked the way. She persuaded him that it was too late and dark to continue and that he had best spend the night in her cottage. There, while he slept, the old woman took the letter from his pocket, opened it and wrote another, imitating the King's writing exactly; and this is what she wrote:

'Immediately you get this letter, you will conduct the bearer of it to our daughter, the Princess. He is our son-in-law and I wish the marriage to take place before my return. Such is my will.'

The Queen, having read this, gave all the necessary orders and took the young man, whom she liked immensely, to the Princess, who took one look at him and fell head over heels in love with him.

When the King returned and learned that the two were married, he was furious. In fact, he lost his temper and swore at the Queen, who became angry too and shoved his own letter under his nose. Sobered, the King asked Plavacek about the old woman, in whose cottage he had spent the night, and from his description realised that she was one of the Fates, and that he had been outwitted.

However, the King was not going to give in so easily, so he said to his son-in-law.

'What's done is done. But still you must earn your position as my son-in-law. Go and get me three golden hairs from the head of Dedewshevede.'

Having said that, he felt confident that he would never see the hated figure of Plavacek again, for Dedewshevede was the sun and no one knew where he lived.

Plavacek went and said good-bye to his wife.

'I've no idea where to find Dedewshevede,' he said, 'but my godmothers, the Fates, will surely know and they'll help me.'

So off he went and the Fates guided his feet so that he went in the right direction and after a long time he came to the shores of the Black Sea. There he saw a ferry-boat with the ferryman sitting in it.

'God bless you, ferryman!'

'And you, young traveller. Where do you want to go?'

'To Dedewshevede's castle to get three of his golden hairs.'

'Well, I'm tired of this job, so if you promise to ask him when I am to get a replacement, I'll take you across.'

Plavacek promised this and the ferryman rowed across to the opposite shore. Travelling on, Plavacek soon came to a large city, lying half in ruins, and there he met a funeral procession. The King of that country was burying his father.

'God console you in your sorrow,' said Plavacek.

'Thank you, good traveller,' said the young King. 'Where are you going?'

'I'm going to Dedewshevede to get three golden hairs.'

'Are you, indeed! I would be grateful, if you could do me a favour. In the palace garden is an apple-tree that used to produce the fruit of Youth, which would restore even a dying man to health and vigour, but for the last twenty years it has not even blossomed. Would you ask Dedewshevede why this is so?'

Plavacek promised and continued on his way. Soon he came to another city, lovely but silent and sad. Near the gate, he encountered an old man hobbling along on a stick.

'God bless you, old man,' said Plavacek.

'And you, too. Where are you going, traveller?'

'I'm going to get three of Dedewshevede's hairs.'

'Indeed, then I must take you to my master, the King.'

'I hear you are going to Dedewshevede,' said the King, 'We have a well here with water that effects miraculous cures; or we had,' and the King sighed, 'but for the last twenty years the well has stood dry, although it never dried out before. Would you ask what the reason is?'

Plavacek promised and continued on his way. He crossed a wide forest and then came to a flowing plain, in which he saw a golden castle and knew that he had reached Dedewshevede's palace. He walked in without encountering anyone: then he saw an old crone squatting in a corner, spinning.

'Greetings, Plavacek, Glad to see you,' she called.

Plavacek recognised her as his godmother, the Fate, who had sheltered him in her cottage.

'What has brought you all this way?' she asked.

'The King won't have me as his son-in-law unless I earn the position and has sent me to get three of Dedewshevede's hairs.'

'Dedewshevede?' she laughed. 'But he's the sun itself, and I'm his mother. Every morning he starts afresh as a baby, becomes a man and in the evening is old and decrepit. I'll get the three hairs for you, but you must not let him see you. Hide under that empty tub there.'

Plavacek then asked if she would ask Dedewshevede the three questions he had promised to put and she said that she would, but that he must listen to the answers and remember them.

All at once a great wind got up, and then, out of the west appeared the sun, a tired old man with a head of golden hair.

'I can smell humans,' he exclaimed. 'Is there anyone here?'

'Who could there be,' replied the Fate. 'You would see anyone even before I did. You're always brushing against humans during the day and must still have the smell of them in your nostrils.'

The old man did not reply, but sat down and had his supper. Then, yawning heavily, he laid his head in his mother's lap and fell asleep.

Seeing him asleep, the Fate took hold of one of his hairs, pulled it out and flung it on the ground. As it fell, it made a twanging sound, like a guitar being plucked.

'What is it, Mother?' asked the old man starting up.

'Nothing, son, I too was asleep and had the strangest dream. I dreamed there was a well somewhere, the waters of which would cure any illness, only for the last twenty years it had stood dry and no one knew how to get the water to rise again.'

'Silly fools,' said the old man. 'There's a frog lodged in the hole through which the spring rises. They've only got to kill the frog, clean the well and the water will rise as before.'

Then he laid his head down again and soon was asleep once more.

The old woman waited a short while, then she pulled out a second golden hair. The old man woke, crying:

'What is it, Mother?'

'Nothing, my son. Only I had another strange dream. I dreamed that there was an apple-tree in some garden, which until twenty years ago used to bear the fruit of Youth, and now the people can't think why it does not even blossom.'

'Silly fools,' said the sun. 'A viper has its home in the tree's roots. Kill that, transplant the tree and it will bear fruit as before.'

A moment later the old man was asleep again. The Fate waited a short while, then pulled out a third hair with a tug that again woke the old man up.

'What is it? Why don't you let me sleep?' he exclaimed angrily.

'Lie still, son,' said the Fate. 'I'm sorry to have disturbed you, but I dreamed there was a ferryman on the Black Sea who said he had been working for twenty years and no one had come to relieve him and he asked me what he should do.'

'Silly fool, he is,' said the sun. 'Why doesn't he shove the oars into the hands of his next passenger, and jump out, then the passenger will have to take over. Now, leave me in peace. I have to get up early, because I must go and dry the tears of the Princess who married the charcoal burner's son. The poor child spends every night crying for her husband, whom her father has told to get three of my hairs.'

The next morning, the Sun got up bright and early, now a handsome child, and set off towards the East. The old woman went and righted the tub under which Plavacek was hiding and gave him the three hairs she had promised him.

'Here are your hairs. Now, you must go. Good luck and a good journey. We shall not meet again, as you will have no further need of me.'

Plavacek thanked her as she deserved and set out back the way he had come.

Reaching the city where the well was, he told the King how to restore its waters and when this worked, the King was so grateful he gave Placavek twelve white horses and as much gold and silver as he could carry.

At the second city, he was able to tell the King how to cure his barren apple-tree and was rewarded with a present of twelve black horses and as many jewels as he could carry.

When he reached the Black Sea, the ferryman asked him if he had any news and, as soon as he had ferried Plavacek and his horses across, Plavacek told him Dedewshevede's answer. The ferryman was overjoyed.

When he reached home, the King could scarcely credit his own good fortune in being the proud possessor of three hairs from the head of Dedewshevede. The young Princess, however, only cared that her husband had returned safely to her.

Later, when his son-in-law told the story of how he had acquired the black and white horses and the great heaps of gold and silver, the greedy King's eyes lit up at the sound of the magic fruit of Youth and the water of the well that cured all ills. He asked his son-in-law how to get there, thinking that if he could just eat one of those apples and sprinkle himself with some of the magic well-water, he would live for ever and so keep Plavacek from ever becoming king. Quickly the King made his preparations and set out on his journey, from which he has not yet returned. It is said that he happened to be the next passenger who used the Black Sea ferry, and that it was into his hands the ferryman thrust the oars, before he jumped overboard and swam ashore. If that is so, then he is probably ferrying people across the Black Sea still.

NINETEEN

Four Brothers

ONCE LONG AGO, a gamekeeper lived with his four sons in a big forest in Bohemia.

As the boys grew up they were dissatisfied with their quiet life and asked their father's permission to go out to seek a trade for themselves. The father gave to each of his sons six gold coins, a suit of new clothes and a hat with a feather in it. He told them that in a year from that day, he would expect them home to say how they had fared and to tell him and each other about their different adventures.

The young men set out and went their separate ways. Each of them went to a different district and each learned a trade. The eldest learned to mend things, the second – I'm afraid to say – learned to be a thief. The third became a star-gazer and the fourth a gamekeeper, like his father. None of these things was so very wonderful or extraordinary, but after a year had passed, the four brothers returned home, well pleased with their achievements.

Their father welcomed them warmly and asked them to tell him of their success. Turning to his eldest son he asked,

'And what sort of trade have you learned?'

'Not one to be very proud of, I fear,' said the eldest son, 'I have just learned to mend things.'

'Oh, for goodness' sake, what a rotten trade to have taken up,' said the father crossly, 'you might have turned your hand to something better.'

'But father, it's not just ordinary mending,' replied the young man, 'for if anything is torn or broken I have only to say, 'let it be mended!' and it is at once as good as new.'

The gamekeeper looked suspicious, but pointing to his torn jacket hanging behind the door he said, 'All right then, mend that!'

'Let it be mended!' said the eldest son and, in a twinkling, the jacket hung there as good as the day it was first made. The father couldn't grumble any more, so he turned to his second son and asked what trade he had learned.

'I'm afraid you'll be ashamed of me, father,' replied the young man, 'for I have learned to be a thief.'

'Ashamed? I should think I am and so should you be ashamed, you worthless fellow!' stormed the angry gamekeeper.

'But, my dear father, I am not just an ordinary thief,' said his second son, 'for I have only to wish some particular thing to come to me and lo! there it is!'

The gamekeeper stared moodily out of the window and just then a stag bounded across a clearing in the trees. 'There you are!' said the father turning quickly, 'you can wish for that stag.'

'Let the stag be here,' said the boy quietly and, to everyone's astonishment, the stag was immediately at their house.

The gamekeeper calmed down and asked his third son to tell them of his new trade.

'You may not be very well pleased,' replied the boy, 'I am just a star-gazer.'

'A star-gazer?' snapped the man, 'and what earthly use will that be to you, may I ask?'

'Oh, but father, I have only to gaze at the night sky and I can see anything, however large or small, anywhere, however near or far, under the stars.' His father hesitated to doubt this after the strange display of his other two sons' powers, so he came at last to his youngest son and asked what trade he had learned.

'I have learned to be a gamekeeper, father,' said the boy.

'Well, at least you have learned something honest and useful,' said his father, 'though why you should have been away a year and travelled far to learn what I could teach you at home, I cannot think.'

'But my dear father, I am not a gamekeeper like you!' cried the boy, 'whatever the quarry, be it large or small, I have only to say 'let it be shot!' and at once it is done.'

The father said, 'I have seen a hare run down the track a minute ago – shoot that, if you can!'

'Let it be shot,' murmured the boy and sure enough the hare fell, but it was too far off to be seen.

'I don't see if it has fallen,' said the father, but his star-gazer son answered, 'Yes, it has, it is just behind those thorn bushes.'

'Let it be here!' said the brother who was the thief, and at once the hare lay in the room, but its skin was torn from being dragged through the thorns.

'Worthless,' said the father grudgingly. 'The pelt is ruined, no one would buy it so torn.'

'Let it be mended!' said the eldest son and in a twinkling the skin of the hare was whole and unblemished.

'Hmm!' muttered the old gamekeeper at last with a twinkle. 'It strikes me that you won't do so badly with the trades you have learned after all!'

So the father and his four sons lived very contentedly together for a while, until news reached them that the King's daughter was lost. The King had promised his crown and the Princess to whoever found her alive and the brothers decided this was just the opportunity for them. The old gamekeeper was reluctant to see his sons go, but they were obstinate and set off on four fine horses, wished for by the second eldest son.

They arrived at the palace, gained audience with the King and told him they were willing to find his lost daughter as long as he promised her hand and his crown to whoever brought her safely home. The King assured them that this was his promise and begged them to find the Princess.

As darkness fell and the night sky was sprinkled with stars, the star-gazer brother gazed at the twinkling heavens and announced that he could see the Princess sitting on an island in the middle of a black lake. She was held there captive by a fierce dragon, who made her stroke his head for two hours each day, while he rested his ugly, scaly head in her lap.

In the morning the brothers set out in a carriage for the black lake, where they embarked in a fishing-boat and sailed to the island. As they drew near to the island, the Princess called to them to make haste, as

the dragon was at that very moment flying back from
raiding a neighbouring kingdom. Seeing the great
beast approaching, the brother who was the thief
cried, 'Let the Princess be here!' and no sooner had
he said these words than the Princess was standing in
the fishing-boat beside them, but sobbing with fright
as the frightful dragon, seeing his fair captive about
to escape, rushed towards them roaring and hissing
with fury. They could hear the approaching clatter
of its great wings when the gamekeeper brother cried
out, 'Let the dragon be shot!' and at once it fell with
a huge splash into the black waters of the lake, which
seethed and boiled and set the boat rocking wildly. As
the dragon fell, its spiked tail thrashed at the boat and
drove a hole through the planks so that the water
poured in and they were in danger of sinking, but the
eldest brother cried, 'Let the boat be mended!' and at
once she was as sound as the day she was built and
bobbing gaily over the waves towards the shore.

Thankfully they all climbed on to dry land and the
brothers helped the beautiful Princess into their waiting carriage and drove in triumph back to the King's
palace. Here they were received with joy and thanks-
giving, but they at once began to quarrel as to which
of them should marry the Princess and be crowned
King. For each of them claimed to have won her by
their special effort. At last they asked the King to
judge which of them had earned the prize.

'My good fellows, you have all earned the prize and
you all deserve her,' said the King, 'but as you cannot
all marry one Princess, I say that the star-gazer shall
be her husband, for without him, the others would not
have been able to know where the Princess was held

prisoner.' (The Princess looked happy at this decision, for the star-gazer really was the most intelligent, as well as the handsomest of the four brothers, the others being a little rough – though worthy – fellows.)

'But,' the King continued, 'in recognition of your services, I shall make each of you the governor of a province.'

So each of the brothers was satisfied with his share of the bargain, and after he had married the Princess, the star-gazer sent for his old father, so that he could share and rejoice in their good fortune.

The old gamekeeper was very impressed by his sons' high positions and pleased by their success. In the spring he stayed with his eldest son, who mended things. In summer with his son who was a thief. In autumn with the gamekeeper and I think that was the time of year that he enjoyed best. But in winter, when snow lay on the ground and the north wind moaned across the land he was well received in the royal home of his son the star-gazer and he warmed his old bones by the palace's roaring fires and watched the young Princes and Princesses – his grandchildren – growing up.